I0518929

# TRUE
# HEART
# REUNION

# TRUE
# HEART
# REUNION

DELORA CONLEY-WALLS

THREE SKILLET

TRUE HEART REUNION, Conley-Walls, DeLora

First Edition


The Reunion Series, Book 3

 THREE SKILLET

www.ThreeSkilletPublishing.com


Cover by Farley L Dunn

All characters are fictitious, and any resemblance to actual persons living or dead is purely coincidental.


This book may not be reproduced in whole or in part, by electronic process or any other means, without permission of the author.

ISBN: 978-1-943189-69-4

Copyright © 2018 by DeLora Conley-Walls
All Rights Reserved

# — 1 —

"GREAT," ROSEMARY BRUTON sighed to no one in particular when she checked the airport's app on her phone and read the notice that her friend Jenny Carleton's plane had encountered bouts of heavy rain. Overhead, the flight number rolled across the display, with the dreaded word: *Delayed*.

She brushed her shoulder-length chestnut hair with her fingers and tucked it behind her, as she glanced warily around the airport at the travelers moving past. She caught sight of herself in a silvered metal panel, and she looked away. Her friends told her she was as attractive as the day she graduated high school, but she saw the lines around her eyes and her mouth that revealed her age.

With her fortieth reunion celebration gearing up,

she was nervous about the people she might see walking through that gate. Her stomach was in knots. At least Jenny was staying with her, and they'd have the chance to catch up on the past year.

She worked her phone into her tailored handbag, with its bronze metal trim and contrasting stitching. Her hand brushed her pocket Bible, and she was reminded of her decision for Christ a little over a year before. She knew her past transgressions were forgiven, but standing in the middle of Pflugerville's Austin Executive Airport, her upcoming reunion kept reminding her of mistakes from four decades earlier. She tried to brush them off and considered heading home for something to eat. Her phone would send her flight updates if the plane made it in before the airport closed.

An exterior door opened as a couple exited, letting the brittle sound of rain inside, and she shivered, recalling the bright days filled with sunshine only the week before. The pelting showers gave the October air a newfound chill. She glanced out the rain-spattered glass to the gloom just beyond, where two planes taxied across the runway. Last week, the temperatures around Pflugerville and her hometown of Round Rock had hovered in the eighties. Today's gloomy weather was forecast to blow out by morning, and she was ready for it to be gone and for the warmth to return.

With optimism, she noted a fresh set of passengers arriving, some in bright, flowered summer wear, possibly from a holiday on the Mexican coast. Two men sported business attire, and one little girl wore a party dress. Rose caught sight of a woman who seemed familiar, one she thought might be arriving for the reunion. Pflugerville was one of the easiest airports to access from Round Rock, and it was likely many attendees would arrive here. The lady was arm-in-arm with a tall man and in an involved conversation, so she didn't call to her.

After about ten minutes, Rosemary headed toward the lone service counter to inquire if her friend's plane might arrive at all that evening. She wasn't sure what her next step should be. She'd tried to reach Jenny on her cell phone, but she hadn't expected to get through if she was onboard. She'd left a message, but it hadn't helped her darkening mood. Other people around her appeared equally irritated and aggravated. From behind her, a loud voice startled her, abruptly bellowing out her name.

"Rose Petal, is that you?"

No! It couldn't be, not that voice, with its deep, unforgettable, resonating sound coming across the airport terminal. She would recognize that man's reverberating, bone-jarring tone anywhere. Thornton Jebulon Wilder. It must be! Despite her astonishment, Rosemary was hardly surprised to be recognized. After having her son Gill, Jr. at twenty-four, she'd maintained her trim figure, and her hair was the same color as in high school, thanks to her awesome stylist. Rose Petal, however, was also from high school, a name that should have stayed in high school, not shouted across the Pflugerville airport. She'd been Rosemary Penndel, and many of her friends had teased her by dropping the Mary and changing her last name ever so slightly. Rose Petal had stuck.

Her eyes skipped across the strangers around her until the man she recognized caught her eye. She let out a sharp breath when her eyes fixed on his broad shoulders and thick head of hair. There was no mistaking Thorn Wilder, a head above the crowd just as she remembered.

How she wished Jenny's plane had arrived on time! Then she'd be gone, and she wouldn't be standing here facing this disaster from her past, one she knew only too well. His dark, penetrating eyes had always been able to see right into her soul. They were the sort of eyes that made others feel as if he was drilling a hole through them and didn't care who knew it.

He was the last person she wanted to see.

Rosemary closed her eyes for a moment, breathed a quick prayer, and then opened them again, hoping beyond hope the moment would magically go away and Thorn would disappear. Yet, his voice was real, and so was his dominating presence.

What was worse, bigger than life itself, Thorn bore down on her, with his eyes locked on her.

"W-why yes, it's me, Thornton. Nice to see you," Rose stuttered, the reality of the moment jerking her roughly back to the present. Indeed, he'd been a literal thorn in her side, and seeing this man wasn't nice at all. A flush of anxiety wrapped warm fingers of dread around her heart. She forced her arm outward and anxiously presented a clammy hand to shake.

As he continued staring, she felt herself grow more apprehensive. Clearly, he was seeing a Rosemary from forty years ago, and it wasn't a look she appreciated. Judging from this brief encounter, Thorn hadn't changed one bit in the past four decades, not in the way he carried himself or his behavior.

After a lengthy pause, he reached his hand as if to shake hers, but just as they touched, he pulled her up close. His warm breath and the faint smell of his cologne took Rose by surprise, and she found his lips on hers before she could push him away. It was all the emotions from high school once again rushing over her in a torrent. As she rose to her tiptoes to meet him, it was as if she had no control of her own.

After the kiss, he gently set her feet back on the terminal floor. Unsettled, her knees weakened with the intensity of the moment, she had trouble getting her balance for the first few seconds. Without thinking, she grabbed his arm. Then, aware of how that small intimacy might seem to others, she placed her hand on his chest and pushed him roughly away. She wouldn't allow her sudden display of emotions to get in the way of keeping her distance from this man.

"Good to see you too, Rose Petal. I can see you're still as sweet as I remember. What was it you said to me the last time we saw each other?" Thorn's deep laugh resonated.

"What do you mean?" Rosemary tried to recall the events of a day she'd worked desperately hard to forget over the past forty years.

"I believe you said come hail or high water, you'd never kiss me again. Well, darlin', there's fixin' to be a flood. You better build you an ark, 'cause you're coming on high water and about to drown!"

With that, Thorn gave a crooked grin, turned heel on his cowboy boots, and strode off, leaving a very bewildered Rosemary standing alone in the airport terminal, as several rows of lights dimmed, and the announcement rang out that the airport was closing in thirty minutes.

# — 2 —

"I WAS HOPING I'd get here first to tell you Thorn was coming to the reunion."

Jenny Carleton, a make-up artist with numerous Hollywood films on her resume, patted her face, flushed from her scramble to exit the airplane after a full night of delays. She luxuriated in the cool air inside the terminal as the words tumbled from her mouth, and there was anticipation on her face as she glanced at Rosemary to gauge her reaction. Outside the building's windows, the morning sun dusted the Hill Country with autumn's glory.

"That would have been nice." Rose gave a shallow smile, one that barely broke the fire-engine perfection of her lips.

"Since we haven't been talking much, I really

didn't want to call and give you such upsetting news over the phone. I thought you might think I was doing it out of spite. He made two reservations on the very first invitation we sent out almost ten months ago. You remember, the *Save the Date* flyer. He paid for his weekend activities then, too." Jenny pursed her lips to cover a smile. Rose unexpectedly meeting Thorn at the airport the night before was a boon she couldn't have anticipated.

They worked toward the baggage pickup section, and it seemed as if every delayed flight had arrived at once. The two women were jostled repeatedly, and it was as if there wasn't a square foot of airport terminal to spare. Part of it was exhaustion. Both women were tired from the chase of resolving yesterday's bad weather issues.

"Two reservations . . . mmm . . . That's more than one, Jenny. Does that mean he's bringing someone with him? Uh . . . he definitely appeared to be alone last night." Rosemary's words stumbled as she recalled the previous evening. "He made such a spectacle of us. I was so embarrassed I almost died right there on the spot."

"Embarrassed?" Jenny reached into her pocketbook and pulled out a mirror, holding it to one eye. She groaned at her smeared mascara.

"You heard me. Maybe more than embarrassed. Humiliated, even." Rosemary began to recount the events of the prior evening to her friend. Her voice was calmer as she reached her hand to tuck a loose strand of hair behind her ear. The small motion, un-thinking and careless, showed her continued tension as she recalled the unexpected meeting and the emotions that had stirred up potent feelings from the past.

"You poor thing." Jenny's eyes caught what Rose's hands were doing. She wished she could have been a fly on the wall to see the encounter. She smiled to herself and quickly stifled it, putting a serious look on her face. She placed her hand on Rose's arm in what she was sure would come across as sincere empathy. "I wish I'd been here to run interference for the two of you. I hate that you had to face him alone. Just to be clear, he definitely made reservations for two for the banquet."

Jenny tried to sound consoling while she thought of the rugged good looks Thorn had once exhibited. At the same time, she wondered if he'd changed much. Every girl in their high school had wanted to be noticed by the "Wild Thorn." His athletic build had dominated all the other boys on the football field, and Jenny couldn't imagine him any other way.

"Were you able to recognize him? Has he changed a whole lot?" Jenny felt certain that Rose hadn't revealed everything from the accidental meeting the previous day.

ROSEMARY BREATHED IN deeply as they slipped Jenny's luggage in her car. She was glad she had something to keep her hands occupied.

"Actually, it's been so long since I've seen him.

He was, I guess, well, if I had to say, he looked even taller and broader than I remembered. He seemed as fit as ever." She paused, closing her eyes. The thoughts running through her head were more than just a memory. This was a reconnection she didn't want to make.

She opened her eyes when Jenny cleared her throat. She shrugged, fighting to keep her voice calm, and whispered, "His hair was definitely different. It was showing silver all around the edges. I saw that up close when he picked me up."

"And? What does that mean?" Jenny smirked.

"He still has those same rough features so many women find attractive, if that's what you're asking." Rose reached for a final valet bag she recognized, understanding the importance of the make-up inside. She carefully worked it in, and she pushed the button on her key fob. She stepped back as the whine of the trunk's motor pulled it gently closed.

"You used to like those features, too, if I remember correctly." Jenny laughed her friend's direction.

Rose jerked her eyes to her friend, her irritation sudden and strong. A few choice words came to her mind, and for a moment, she wished this reunion weren't taking place at all. She didn't need these jabs. Perhaps meeting Jenny hadn't been such a good idea.

Then, biting her lip and looking away, she took a deep breath, and she sensed her new-found faith in God reminding her of the pastor's sermon the previous week. Control of her tongue was vital to her

Christian witness. Anyway, what Jenny said was true. That was what pained her. She knew every word was exactly the way she remembered it. That didn't mean she wanted to be reminded of it.

"That was a long time ago, and a lot of muddy water's disappeared under that bridge. More than I care to remember. Let's not bring all that up. I want to enjoy this reunion despite Thorn."

JENNY KNEW WHEN to stop. Rose's agitated sigh sent her a very clear message. As kids, they'd tormented each other unmercifully. However, since high school, Rose hadn't been able to take being pushed. She would just balk and do nothing at all, distancing herself from the situation, even cutting off her friends. Jenny had long ago learned that when Rose became too irritated, only a sincere apology—as well as the offer of a facial or makeover—would get through her shell.

That was what had happened last year when Jenny had asked Rose an innocent question about several events from their high school years. Rose had found the questions nosy, and she had cut Jenny off, refusing to answer her entreaties for reconciliation. Jenny had waited for her to calm down, hoping for a response, but after a year, with the reunion looming, Jenny had been forced to break the ice without Rose's help.

"I'm with you all the way, Rose," Jenny began, hoping to smooth her friend's newly ruffled feathers.

Before she could offer more than the barest support, Rose interrupted her.

"I don't even want to go to the reunion, now that I know the 'Wild Thorn' will be there." She glanced at Jenny, her eyes red with emotion. "But if I don't go, I'll miss seeing all the old friends I do care about. I feel like he's trying to cause trouble for me. You know that if I go, I'll have to deal with him. But if I don't, I'll feel like he ran me off just like he did after high school." Rose reached for a tissue to blow her nose.

"Of course you're going to the reunion. Don't let Thorn scare you away." Jenny was very determined, and while she intended to be supportive, she intended to convince Rose to attend this reunion, no matter what, especially since Thorn would be there. She would side with Rose, because their friendship needed repairing, even skipping some of the reunion's scheduled events, if necessary, but that wasn't her plan, and it was entirely too early to give up now, even though she was certain Rose would weaken and try to back out later. That just meant Jenny had to put more effort into it.

Besides, she was interested in how Thorn had turned out after all these years. If he was anything like Rose had described him from their brief encounter at the airport, he couldn't have changed much and must be as attractive as ever.

"Oh, I won't," Rose assured her. "I just wish Gill was here with me. He was always so supportive." She drooped in her seat, her emptiness at the loss of her husband draining her for a moment. "I really miss him at times like this."

Jenny nodded that she understood. Rose's husband had died from a stroke only three years before. However, despite Rose's wish for her husband at her side, Jenny knew she had been dominated by him. Gill had been an extremely possessive man. It had taken every effort for her to become as independent as she was now.

The unspoken truth was that if Gill were still alive, Rose might not be allowed to attend the reunion. He had maintained a tight rein over her, and he was always looking for an excuse to be jealous. Jenny had realized that after the first time she met him. He hadn't been comfortable with the two women talking about their high school years. He hadn't wanted his wife mentioning anything about her life from before their marriage. Jenny was certain he'd felt threatened by any man from Rose's past, but especially Thornton Wilder.

Rose and Jenny arrived about ten minutes later at Rose's picturesque Austin stone home just outside of town, hers since shortly after Gill died. The rugged terrain made the homes in the area blend into the environment, and being outside town, deer roamed the yard. Her old house had too many memories tied to it, and she'd let it go as quickly as possible.

Jenny put her things in the main guest room, glad to see that it had a private bath. She loved the antique furniture, and especially the elegant brass bed that accompanied this room. The bed and furnishings had belonged to Rose's great-grandmother, Doris. Being here made her feel like she was at a very stylish bed and breakfast.

"Do your son and his wife stay here when they visit?" Jenny walked into the family room to find Rose drinking a glass of water. On the table were her vitamins and supplements. She stepped to her friend and picked up her vitamin bottle to see just what she was taking now. She looked at her with raised eyebrows and laughed. "Silver vitamins? Honey, you need the titanium bottle."

Rose chuckled and took the bottle from her, moving it and all the rest to the back of the table. "And you keep your hands off my supplements. To answer your question about my son and his wife, sometimes they stay with me, and other times they insist on a hotel. I think it's more for their privacy than mine. I have plenty of room for them and the two grandbabies, well, they're not grandbabies, any longer. However, even when I insist otherwise, Junior and Evelyn always feel like they're intruding in my life."

Jenny plopped into a comfortable chair. "Do you prefer for them to stay here?" She smiled at the softness of the cushions, running one hand down the arm.

"I ENJOY HAVING them near me. It was Gill who wanted his privacy. He was always so possessive, even when it came to his own son. He was jealous of anyone taking my time away from him." Rose smiled, remembering the times her children and grandchildren had spent with her both before and after Gill's death. Before he had died, they'd been a breath of fresh air. Afterwards, she'd welcomed the company.

"Then you should always insist on them staying with you. This is such a wonderful place that I wouldn't stay anywhere else, if I were invited." Jenny crossed her legs and bounced one foot in the air contentedly, certain her friend would get the hint.

Rose sighed and picked up one of her vitamin bottles to peruse the label absently. "It should be that easy, Jenny. Looking back, I realize Gill could be an extremely selfish man at times. But I didn't have many men to judge him by, since my father was in the military and always gone. I liked the fact that Gill was around and wanted me near him. It wasn't until later in our marriage that I realized how controlling he was." Rose paused, then continued with a brighter tone. "The kids all stayed with me the last time they were down, so perhaps they'll be here more in the future. Gill, Jr. knows I want him here, but old insecurities and habits are hard to break."

"I'm glad you've made them feel welcome. With any luck, this will be where they come from now on." Jenny glanced at her watch, frowning.

"What, Jenny?" Rose saw the look at the watch. "Surely you can't have an appointment for a facial so soon after arriving in town." She winked, teasing her friend. It really was good to have her staying in her home with her.

Jenny smiled at Rose, and she held out one arm, patting the inside crook of her elbow. "I've been on the plane since early this morning and haven't eaten. I must keep my insulin levels in mind, because my sugar level could drop at any time. Diabetes. Type two. At least I don't have to stick my arm, just maintain my illness by regular food intake. My waist line doesn't like it, but my taste buds sure do." She stood, reaching for her purse. "Are you hungry? How about us grabbing a bite for breakfast? It'll be my treat."

"Breakfast, huh? Is that how you do it?" Rose looked at her friend for a minute, amazed that this friend of hers could eat a regular breakfast and still manage to hang on to her beautiful looks four decades out of high school, diabetes or not. Maybe there was a trick she could pick up there.

"Do what, Sweetie?" Jenny dangled her purse, missing the point altogether. "Ready?"

Rose laughed, standing to gather her things. Jenny was a guest. Of course, she would go. "Breakfast, it is. I completely forgot about your blood sugar. Where do you want to eat? The Big Griddle serves a great breakfast, if that's what you're thinking, or there's a buffet in the hotel downtown."

Rose grabbed her purse and moved toward the door, her fingers working the house alarm. She held the door for Jenny as they headed out to the car, their conversation already on which restaurant they would choose.

# — 3 —

THORN IDLED HIS truck into the parking space and peered at the cars in the lot. The first thing he'd done upon taking possession of his rental was put Rose's address in the navigation system. Her address on the destination bar called to him, and he forced himself to look away. He killed the engine and let his eyes rest on the car next to him. At the airport last night, there'd been one just like it parked next to him. Rose's? He thought it looked like one she'd drive.

He wondered if he'd see her inside.

The reputation of the establishment was the best in town, and if she was eating breakfast in Round Rock, this is where she'd be. Taking a deep breath, he unlatched his door, climbed down, and headed inside.

The hostess offered him a choice of a secluded table or a booth that was more open. He asked her to give him a moment, letting his eyes roam the seated clientele. He smiled to himself when he saw Rose, the source of his night of insomnia. Across from her sat Jenny Carleton. A waitress was just leaving the table. Things were falling into place quicker than he'd anticipated.

THE WOMEN HAD chosen a booth with large, sweeping views of the dining room. Rose had ordered orange juice and black coffee, while Jenny requested coffee with French vanilla-flavored creamer, along with a large glass of milk. Asking for a minute to select from the menu, they were engrossed in the choices when a deep voice interrupted them.

Rose's head immediately shot up to see Thorn's football-player frame looming over them. Her heart began to pound, and irritation—or something she could later claim as irritation—surged through her.

Thorn was intruding on her space once again.

"Mornin'." Thorn's eyes were bloodshot as if he'd been up all night, but at least he was clean-shaven and faintly smelled of soap and cologne. Without asking her permission, he announced, "Move over, Rose Petal."

Rose was taken aback. How dare he! Even as she raged inside, she felt his kiss from the airport as the same unwelcome emotions swept back over her. It was happening again; she felt herself enveloped by this man who had loved and left her.

"I don't guess I own the restaurant, do I?" Her hand involuntarily squeezed the menu, crushing one corner. She quickly put it aside. In disbelief, she found herself scooting down to allow Thorn to sit.

She cringed inside, furious at the control he still exerted over her. All he had to do was walk back into her life, and she caved. She should be strong around this man, and that was something she hadn't done well so far.

Thorn filled the booth with his considerable six-foot-four height and broad shoulders. Then he leaned his elbows on the table and looked at Jenny.

"Well, hello, I-Dream-of-Jeanie."

"NICE TO SEE you, too," Jenny shot back, finishing with, "Thorn Bird!" She was surprised by his bold actions, just waltzing up and making himself at home with the two of them. And to think, she'd even looked forward to seeing him again.

Now she wasn't so sure.

She wondered if he'd even considered they might not want his company. It was clear he still had his daring good looks, and it didn't seem like he'd changed all that much in the last forty years. There were a few laugh lines crinkling around his eyes and mouth, and his skin was deeply tanned. That probably meant he still worked outside as he'd done as a teenager. She did notice one discrepancy in Rose's description of him. His hair that was "silver at the edges" was rich and sleek, burnished with a metallic sheen, and showing only traces of a well-remembered auburn sprinkled through it.

Before Thorn had time to remark about Jenny's less-than-enthusiastic greeting, the waitress returned with the women's drinks. In his rumbling voice, Thorn ordered black coffee as well and told the waitress to return in a minute for his breakfast selection.

ROSE WISHED SHE'D just gotten up and left the restaurant. Yet, it was as if Thorn could read her mind.

"This is quite a surprise running into you twice in less than twenty-four hours, when I haven't seen you in almost forty years. I certainly wasn't prepared for this rendezvous." He nodded at both Jenny and Rose. Then, with a quick motion, he reached and tapped Rose's nose with the tip of one finger.

She felt a current go through her like a lightning bolt. It was a motion she remembered well, and she'd enjoyed it as a teen. Now, however, he needed to keep his hands off. He simply looked at her and winked, making her even more uncomfortable. She was determined to run at the slightest provocation— or open space at the table. Oh, if she wasn't trapped between the wall and this man!

Rose took a deep breath when the waitress returned to take their order, placing a cup of black coffee in front of Thorn. It gave her a distraction from what he'd done. With abandon, she pointed to the French toast on the menu, unable to force herself to say what she wanted. Her brain was crazy with the man next to her, remembering old sentiments and wanting him gone at the same time. In her heart, she didn't care if she had French toast, or if the waitress brought her nothing at all. With Thorn next to her, she didn't think she could keep anything down.

"I THINK MY friend wants the French toast." Jenny took Rose's menu and handed it to the waitress. She brightly ordered the Garden Omelet Breakfast, winking at Rose. Anyone could see that the poor woman was uncomfortable, and it had all started with Thorn's sudden presence at their table. She covered her giggle with her hand, hoping Rose didn't notice.

THORN ORDERED THE Simple Breakfast, which included two eggs, bacon, toast and hash browns. He hadn't slept the previous night, and the pounding in his temples had only gotten worse with the rising of the sun. He needed fuel, and he needed it quickly. He even found it hard to respond with good humor when the waitress flirted shamelessly with him. After she stepped away, he raised the coffee to his lips, closing his eyes and drawing in the aroma. It was what he needed to perk up his morning.

"WELL, I CAN definitely tell you haven't changed that much." Jenny laughed, chiding Thorn, thinking how many girls had liked him in high school and hadn't minded letting him know. He'd garnered quite a reputation for being the man to chase.

"Hey, I had nothing to do with what happened all those years ago." Thorn grinned, finally brightening with a sip of his coffee. He pushed a package of sugar around the table with his finger. "Women are just cinnamon mocha to me. They show up, and the aroma draws me in. I can't help it if I still have that animal magnetism so many women crave." He rolled his eyes as he said it, letting Jenny know he was teasing. Taking another sip from his cup, he turned his eyes to Rose, "You weren't jealous there for a moment, were you?"

ROSE'S EYES FLASHED. This was too much!

"Jealous? Should I be? Is there a reason for me to be jealous of that woman?" Her words snapped at Thorn like a rattlesnake.

Thorn smiled even broader.

"Still the same Rose Petal, never letting anyone know how she feels until it's too late." Despite his smile, his voice had a bitter edge to it. He drummed his fingers on the table, and the bantering fell quiet.

Now, what was that supposed to mean? Rose thought to herself. She could feel Thorn watching her intently, but she sat in stony silence. She wouldn't try to engage him in polite conversation. She wanted breakfast to be over and Thorn to be gone.

JENNY, HOWEVER, WAS of a different persuasion. She had begun enjoying Thorn's company, even if she knew Rose was piqued. She laughed brightly, reaching to tap the man's arm, as she chatted about her life over the last forty years. Her words paused from time to time for the appropriate oohs and aahs from Thorn when describing various parts of her relationships with her family.

Then, Jenny changed directions, asking about some of the wild antics Thorn was accused of pulling in high school. Hanging his head at some, and smiling gleefully at others, he admitted to most of them. Jenny even questioned Rose about an incident or two, but her friend was less than forthcoming. At each prompt, she simply gave a little cough and tried to keep the conversation centered on Jenny. It was obvious she didn't want her past mentioned, especially not with Thorn sitting at her side.

THEN, THANKFULLY, THEIR food arrived, and for a time, Rose could relax. There was no additional discussion about Rose's past or Thorn's rapscallion behavior.

Thorn dug into his Simple Breakfast, and Jenny had no trouble attacking her omelets. The same wasn't true for Rose, who did no more than nibble her French toast. It was too much of a struggle to eat with Thorn sitting so close.

Finally, Rose dropped her toast onto her plate and sighed, certain that Thorn was gradually moving her direction. By this time, she felt he was practically in her lap.

"DOES THE FRENCH toast taste bad?" Thorn pointed at Rose's plate. He noticed she'd only eaten one of the four slices.

She turned her eyes to him, pushing the plate his direction. "I'm really not much of an eater in the morning. Coffee and juice usually are enough for me until lunch."

"Oh, they are, are they? So that's how you've kept your trim waist." He grinned, then he reached his fork across her plate and cut off a piece of the toast for himself. He dipped it in her syrup and bit off one end, chewing it slowly and thoughtfully.

"Hmm, not bad," he said and extended his arm for another bite.

JENNY WATCHED IN astonishment. This was just like in high school. Thorn had always sat with Rose and eaten off her tray. Well, and everyone else's, too, but that was beside the point. He was still doing it, and from the look on Rose's face, she didn't like it one bit. She just wanted this ordeal to be over.

Jenny fought a smile. It was too cute for words.

"How'd you sleep last night, Rose Petal?" After his third bite of French toast, Thorn looked at Rose with a wink. Then he chuckled. "Did you rest well?"

"I . . . I slept fine, except for worrying about Jenny's flight being delayed until this morning," she replied.

"Well, I thought maybe that little good night kiss

you gave me might have kept you awake," Thorn shot back at her, and he turned so only Jenny could see his face. A grin appeared, and it was clear the jab had been intentional.

"THORNTON JEBULON WILDER, I in no way initiated that kiss!" Rose raised her voice at him, as her skin turned hot with anger. He wasn't going to blame that incident on her. "I had nothing to do with that, and you know it. I didn't even notice you in the terminal. You recognized me first."

Thorn chuckled. "Well, I guess there was that chance I might have been mistaken, I admit. I wasn't sure it was you, you looked so trim. I'd have expected your long ponytail and bobby socks, you know. Now your hair hangs barely below your neck and your legs look—"

HE DIDN'T GET a chance to finish before he was interrupted by a warm-sounding hello from a former classmate and friend, Roxanne. The warmth covered an ulterior motive, though. She'd seen Thorn from across the room and had waited to be sure it was him. She'd carried a crush on him in high school, along with every other available female. Even so, he'd always been with Rose Petal.

"Hey, Jenny and Thorn. When did you arrive?" Thorn's massive bulk had blocked Rose from view, and now Roxanne was surprised to see a third person at the table, and even more stunned to find that it was

Rosemary.

It was too bad things had never worked out for them after high school, she thought to herself. They should have had each other.

"HEY, BEAUTIFUL!" Thorn stood up to give Roxanne a big hug, and then he pointed across the table, telling her to sit down by Jenny. With a chuckle, he returned to his spot by Rose, gruffly apologizing for the lack of space. It didn't stop him from sliding right up against her, though. All Rose could do was sit there and pretend it didn't affect her, but she could feel her pulse race. She wanted to think it was anger, but it felt too much like emotions she'd expunged decades before, back when she and Thorn were together.

She didn't like this at all. She vowed to find a way to exit as soon as she saw a chance.

"How are you doing, Rose?" Roxanne stretched her arm across the table and offered it to her. "I didn't see you there next to your old beau." A wink to Thorn accompanied her words.

"I ARRIVED LAST night, and Jenny just got here this morning." Thorn pretended to take no notice of Rose's reaction to him. However, he could read her like a book. She wasn't hiding anything from him.

"When Jack and I spoke to Rosemary at church last Sunday, she didn't tell me you were coming to the reunion," Roxanne continued. "Did you, Rose?"

"She didn't know, because I wanted to surprise her," Thorn revealed smoothly. "She and I have a lot of catching up to do." With that comment he reached over and patted Rose's hand, smiling.

ROSE KNEW IT wasn't a real smile. Thorn was up to something. She just didn't know what. Her gut instinct told her one thing for certain:

She was going to find out, whether she wanted to or not.

# — 4 —

WHILE THEY WERE enjoying breakfast, Thorn didn't bother to mention to Rose he'd been up all night after their chance meeting in the airport terminal. He hadn't expected to see his Rose Petal there, and he'd been shaken to his core by her appearance. That night after reaching his hotel room, he hadn't been able to sleep no matter how hard he tried.

He'd planned to see her and confront her at the reunion that weekend, so he could finally have closure. Afterward, it would be over between them forever. The airport terminal changed all that. Rose Petal had been searching the faces around her. Seeing her had brought back all the old memories, and impulsively, he'd swept her up and kissed her.

He hadn't been able to help himself. It was as

natural as breathing to him. All the years of anguish and torment had seemed to wash away in that one instant when he finally saw Rose and called out her name. After forty years, he'd been caught up in the aroma of her perfume, and it had taken him to a time he'd thought forgotten.

She hadn't pulled away—or at least she hadn't rejected him out of hand. That had been a surprise. He'd expected her to lash out at him, to berate him verbally when he grabbed her.

If he could believe what his parents had told him about their last meeting with her, he had expected her to call security. He clung desperately to the knowledge she hadn't turned him away, instead giving in to his embrace.

Even so, he'd come for the reunion this weekend to erase her memory from his life forever, not to rekindle an old romance. He'd been certain that his youth and lack of experience had made that long-ago Rose appear more desirable than she really was. He'd hoped to find a woman who was just someone he'd known back in high school, someone he wouldn't look at twice if he saw her walking down the street.

He was so wrong. In that short five minutes in the airport, he'd been reminded just how beautiful she really was to him.

Now, at the restaurant, just to be sitting beside her in the same booth. This wasn't some high school boy's crush. This was an all-out addiction, and the only way to cure it was to get more of Rose.

Yet, the reality of his life pulled at him. He couldn't turn loose of the last forty years so easily. He'd been a mess since high school, and all because of Rose. No matter how much he felt the old attraction, he wouldn't give in to it. She'd been the cause of all his years of unrest and unhappiness.

As he gazed at her, doubts clouded his thoughts. He'd done his best to forget her. Alcohol, other women, and even a military tour of duty across the farthest parts of the globe hadn't erased her from his mind. He reminded himself that she'd betrayed their love and ultimately destroyed their brief marriage. Thorn's father was a two-star general at the time. His parents had warned him about Rose, but he'd been stubborn. They said she was just using him to get her father, a sergeant, a promotion, but that didn't matter to Thorn. He'd loved Rose, no matter her father's rank. Then she'd turned out to be just what Thorn's parents had claimed her to be.

Still, sitting next to her was magic.

Thorn finished eating and sat morosely, staring at an empty plate. Next to him, equally miserable, Rose did her best to ignore him. Roxanne rambled on about her husband Jack, her hand flitting through the air, emphasizing her every word, telling about how he was planning to attend the reunion as well. It was when she reached to touch Thorn on the wrist with the tips of her fingers that he could take no more. Without warning, he stood and said his good-byes. Rose breathed an audible sigh of relief when she realized he intended to leave her friends and her in peace.

Thorn frowned. He knew his presence had made an impact on her. He couldn't be certain whether it was a positive or a negative one, not unless he based it on her response at the airport. That brought a smile to his face; maybe she'd had a difficult time forgetting him, too. It was a comforting but fleeting thought. If she'd really missed him, she would have done something about it long before now.

He set his jaw in a stubborn line, irritation eating at his heart. It was the remains of an old love, one that had yet to be extinguished. It had burned low over the years, sometimes pushed out of mind, but never cold. No, never cold. He realized it wasn't cold now, as much as he hoped it would be.

"I guess you'll have to wait until later to see me again." As he said his teasing words, Thorn reached for Rose's hand and kissed it. He lifted his eyes to see her cringe and look away.

Refusing to be goaded, he picked up the tab for the three women and left a too-generous tip.

IN ROSE'S MIND, Thorn's tip was excessive for a waitress who had flirted way too much, and she made it known with narrowed eyes and pursed lips. Thorn snorted in amusement, and even that irritated her.

As for the kiss, she knew he was just showing off to Jenny and Roxanne. He didn't care for her, and she knew it. She didn't know what he was trying to prove by giving her so much attention.

She intended to find out, though, before Thorn pulled some stunt that really embarrassed her.

# — 5 —

"GIRL, I THINK he has it as bad for you as he ever had." Jenny put her hand on Rose's. Her eyes crinkled, and there was laughter in her voice.

"Amen to that, sister!" piped in Roxanne. "I know every rose has its thorn, but this is ridiculous. He couldn't keep his hands off you. It was like he'd never touched a woman before. He was behaving just like he did in high school, and maybe worse." Both women giggled at Rose. She shifted in her seat, uncomfortable with their comments, and her irritation showing in her dark looks.

"No, girls. You must be mistaken. Thorn can't stand me. He's just doing this as some kind of test or show." Rose tightened her mouth in memory of what had happened at the airport. "Last night he even told me, 'There's fixing to be a flood,' so I don't think this is about love at all."

She cringed at the other things that had happened at the airport, but she couldn't share that with the women across from her. Nothing made sense to her. She hadn't understood what had happened between Thorn and her all those decades ago, but now she was more confused than ever. What kind of trick was he trying to pull? He'd made it abundantly clear years before that he wanted nothing to do with her. So why the big show of affection now? This wasn't what Rose had expected on her fortieth class reunion. She'd been looking forward to visiting with old classmates, not being mauled, manhandled, and in-sulted by Thorn.

She'd always felt an emptiness and void after her break-up with Thorn. She'd been praying for a change in her life. Then along had come Gill. She'd tried to fill the void inside with her new husband, and later with Gill, Jr., among other things. Vacations, a new house, and later a series of expensive cars had all given her momentary fulfillment. It had seemed to work for a while. A few times she thought she was over Thorn.

Now that she was alone, she felt the emptiness more than ever.

As the appeal of each new thing in her life faded, she'd often asked God what her purpose was. She would tell him that she needed something more, hope she could wrap her days around, an interest that could fulfill her. Her answer hadn't come, not in forty years, and she was certain Thorn wasn't it now.

This must be a test to see if she really did trust God to be in control of her life. Either that or it was a test to see if she believed in true love. Either way, Rose wasn't happy that Thorn was back in town, even if it was only for a few days. She could have lived another four decades without seeing him. Driving Jenny back to her house, Rose was confident that any attraction for Thorn she might have felt at the airport wouldn't return.

She would see to that.

JENNY WAS TOTALLY shocked by Thorn's behavior as well. There had been rumors after high school, but Rose never spoke about it, and Jenny never asked. Rose would come unglued at the mention of Thorn. One rumor said that he and Rose had gotten married. Another said she had his love child. Some people suggested Rose dumped Thorn for reasons unknown.

What little Jenny knew had come from a hysterical Rose a long time ago. It seemed the bad blood between the couple had happened after both their parents were transferred to different military bases. Rosemary's family ended up in Germany, while Thorn's family was stationed in Japan.

Jenny knew this much: That was when Thorn had signed up. His parents tried to stop him. His father pulled rank to garner stateside postings, but he went abroad anyway, volunteering for the most dangerous missions. He made it back all in one piece, never to return to their old hometown.

Jenny shrugged Thorn off. Other people's lives had changed, just like his. She'd lived away for a while now, too. Her two brothers had both moved away, as well. Andy and his wife Pauline lived in the next town, about thirty minutes away, and when she told Rose she planned to see him after the reunion was over, Rose said she thought it would be nice to see them again, if Jenny didn't mind her tagging along. Jenny was pleased. After seeing Thorn over the reunion weekend, Rose would definitely need a distraction.

Andy was a couple of years older and had three children. Only his youngest child, a nineteen-year-old daughter, still lived at home with him and his wife. Her brother had liked Rosemary when she first started high school. When she and Jenny had become friends, he had been even more enthusiastic about going out with her. He was already a junior, and their relationship didn't last more than a few dates. Despite that, they had remained friends.

They made plans for Sunday afternoon to drive over and visit for a few hours before Jenny had to catch her plane.

AT LEAST THEY thought that was the plan. Their only problem was they hadn't run it by Thorn, who had made a few plans of his own.

All his plans included Rose, whether she was prepared or not, and all her plans would have to be put aside.

Thornton Jebulon Wilder was back in town.

# — 6 —

ROSE FOUGHT TO wake as she lay in her bed.

It was early Friday morning, and a recurring dream had haunted her night. She was still a teenager in the dream, and it was always the same. She heard a baby crying, and the doctor said it was a girl.

Then everything was silent.

It wasn't a nightmare, but like someone was lost. She would wake in a hospital or in a room of solid white and be completely alone. She wasn't afraid, but she always knew something was missing. She never could put her finger on it, but she knew something wasn't right.

It always made her sad as she thought about her own losses.

Pushing the dream aside, she yawned. It was an

old one, and she needed to get up, get a shower, and start her busy day. She had to get her hair and nails done before the barbeque. The pavilion had been reserved at the lake, and some of the local classmates were setting up grills and doing ribs and brisket at noon. The picnic, however, wasn't until five-thirty. She was responsible for potato salad for thirty and three lemon meringue pies.

Since Jenny was from out of town, she would be bringing chips and dip and ice for the tea. This would be the casual family gathering. Everyone was invited. Tomorrow night was the banquet, and only the reunion couples would be allowed to attend. Rose had already bought a cute overall short set to wear today. She pulled it out of the closet to show Jenny and get her opinion, certain her friend would approve.

"THAT MAKES YOU look too skinny and too old." Jenny held up the short set next to Rose. "It's at least two sizes too big. Don't you have some denim shorts and a tank top?"

Rose was shocked at the idea of wearing a tank top at her age. Gill had been so jealous that she never bought anything that was form fitting or revealing in any way.

"No, I really don't wear shorts much. Usually just capris."

"Well," Jenny quipped, grabbing the bag the clothing had come in, "before we do another thing, we're taking this back to the store and trading it for something a little fashionable, something that looks good on you."

Jenny sounded like she was making plans for Rose's clothes, and Rose wasn't sure she liked that. The first part of the morning was spent finding something they could both agree on. Jenny wanted Rose to look like a fashionista, while Rose was still selecting clothes too loose for her. Finally, they compromised on a turquoise tank top covered by a matching lace blouse. They paired that with fitted black denim shorts that came down to the top of her knees. Then Jenny talked Rose into buying a strappy black sandal with chunky turquoise stones on them. The overall look was fresh but not too flirty.

Jenny accompanied Rose to her hair appointment. She had Rose's hairstyle transformed to a wispy look from the staid uniform style to which she was accustomed. She had the nail girl apply acrylic nails on Rose's long fingers, and along with her toenails, paint them a creamy orange sherbet. By early afternoon, Rose felt as if she'd experienced a complete makeover.

On the way home, Jenny bought chips, dip and ice. Over the next few hours, they worked until they had the food ready, preparing the potato salad and the pies.

Then Jenny volunteered to do Rose's make-up. That felt like the last straw.

"I don't know what you're trying to do, but I don't like it. I'm me, Rosemary Josephine Bruton, not some runway model. I think I still know how to do my own make-up," Rose snapped harshly, immediately regretting her words. Her upsetting evening and her morning with Thorn had worn her nerves to a frazzle.

"I'm sorry, Rose. It's just that you look so incredible, I thought maybe some of my colors of lipstick and blush might bring out your skin tones better with your new clothes." Jenny sounded truly remorseful. Rose felt a little sheepish at her own dramatic display of annoyance. Jenny was just trying to help, like she always did, and since she did this professionally, it probably wouldn't hurt.

"Oh, I suppose so. Do what you can." Rose let out a defeated sigh. She never wore a lot of make-up, just a little mascara, lipstick, and a good moisturizer. Jenny always looked so well put together and stylish. It might even be fun.

"Great! Let's get to work," came Jenny's eager reply, as she began working on the contours of her friend's face. In just a matter of minutes, Rose could not believe the transformation. Her eyes seem to jump out and sparkle, while her new rich lip color seemed to invite an engaging response. She didn't look like the Rose everyone expected. This was a new improved version!

"Wow! Even I don't recognize myself." Rose smiled as she gazed into the mirror. She looked softer, and dare she think it? Even somewhat appealing. Just the right make-up with the perfect clothes to complete her look.

At least that was what Jenny told her. They packed their things in the car and headed for the picnic and a reunion neither of them would soon forget.

# — 7 —

ROSE AND JENNY arrived at the barbeque picnic just as the food was being brought to the tables, and they were drawn in by the pungent aroma of the meat the local men had been smoking all day. Rose put her potato salad next to Roxanne's pasta salad. Then she carried her pies to the dessert area while Jenny took her ice to the beverage center.

Rose turned around at a low whistle and saw Jack and Roxanne both staring at her.

"Girl, when you clean up, you clean up good! Where was this Rose forty years ago?" Roxanne walked up to her, reaching a hand to touch her hair, and she took Rose's chin in her fingers and studied her face. She smiled to show how much she approved.

"Uhh, hmm," came approving sounds from Jack.

"Husband, watch it!" Roxanne poked him in the ribs.

"I was just agreeing with you, Roxie. That was all, honey," he said weakly. At the same time, he winked at Rose, causing her to laugh.

"Jack, you're such a character! I don't know how Roxanne's put up with you all these years," Rose teased, in a mock-reproving tone.

"Unfortunately for me, it's true love," Roxanne admitted. She reached up and gave Jack a kiss on the cheek. "Maybe someday I'll get over him, but not today." They laughed as they strolled off arm in arm together.

For a moment Rose looked at them with envy. They had been married for over thirty years and were still in love. Roxanne hadn't been an angel in high school, but when she went off to college and met Jack, she had come back and seemed to have been happy ever since.

Rose knew what had made the difference. The transformation in Roxanne had occurred when Jack introduced her to his personal savior, Jesus Christ. They'd married, and she'd taught school while Jack coached. Together they raised their two sons. They were involved in church, and their boys were respectful young adults. Rose was still staring wistfully in their direction, when she heard a voice from behind her, startling her ever so slightly.

"Would'a, could'a, should'a."

She could tell it was Thorn before she ever turned around. She knew he'd seen her watching Roxanne and Jack, and she wondered how long he'd been standing behind her. As she turned around to make eye contact, she heard the air in his lungs escape in a hollow gasp.

THORN COULDN'T BELIEVE his eyes. Rose had never looked more beautiful in all the time he'd known her. She'd been a naturally attractive girl in high school. But seeing her dressed like this was overwhelming. Her trim outfit set off her hair, and her flawless make-up made her face come alive. He could smell just a hint of perfume, and suddenly, he couldn't even remember that girl from high school. In front of him stood a woman who knew how to use the beauty God had given her. He breathed in deeply trying to soak in her loveliness.

Then, just as suddenly, a nagging thought slipped in. Why was she dressed like this today? She was either with someone, or she was waiting for someone to arrive. She'd never dress like this for herself.

He didn't want to see Rose with anyone but him, he admitted to himself, as if trying to face some awful truth. He tried to push away the seed of jealousy he felt deep within his heart and tried to reassure himself. He had a purpose this weekend, and it was one that was forty years in the making. What could he be thinking? Old feelings didn't matter. He didn't want Rose. He didn't care about her. She could do whatever she pleased. It wouldn't matter one bit to him.

He fought to hold on to that, even as he felt it slipping away. He took a deep breath, accepting that reality was reality. His determination to be strong wasn't working. He was jealous that Rose might be with any other man than him at the reunion.

"Thorn, are you listening?" Rose interrupted his thoughts.

"What, Rose Petal?" Thorn fought to remember what he'd been saying.

"I ASKED WHAT you just said to me, but never mind. If you don't remember, I certainly don't care." Rose turned to leave the dessert area. She had no time for this man. Sleepless nights and a kiss in the airport were certainly no cause for her to change her opinion of him after all these years.

Thorn glanced at the baked confections, his eyes stopping on the pies. "Did you make the lemon meringue pies?"

"Yes," Rose replied, in a curt, indifferent tone. She had no need for his questions, but it was an innocent one that she would answer for anyone who asked.

"I remember the time you made one just for me. It was right after—" He was interrupted by a loud voice yelling at him from across the park.

"Thorn, is that you?"

Thorn looked with irritation to see who was calling to him. It was one of his old high school buddies,

Bobby Edwards. Bobby hurried over to shake Thorn's hand, and then he noticed Rose.

"Well, I see it's still true. Every Rose has its Thorn, even if it's a wild one." He caught up Rose in a hug and planted a kiss on her forehead. Rose smiled and patted his arm. Thorn frowned at the display of affection, but Bobby didn't seem to notice.

"I read about your husband in the paper a few years back. I'm sorry for your loss, Rose. Even though I live in Austin now, I still take the *Leader* to keep up with events around here. It makes me feel like I'm still connected."

IT WAS MORE than that. Bobby was into politics, and he liked to keep his hand on the pulse of the people he represented. He worked hard to be the sort of representative his people needed. Besides that, a photo or two taken with him and the people, to be seen with his constituents, was always good for politics. The *Round Rock Leader*, the local paper, would be happy to publish an article about their elected representative being back for a homecoming reunion.

He had to be careful, though. Rose was entirely too appealing today, and he wouldn't want to be photographed with her at the picnic. The rumors might start flying in Austin. He and his wife lived a very upscale lifestyle, and they needed to keep a low profile.

Bobby smiled broader, entranced by Rose, and beside him, a frown creased Thorn's brow.

"Is your wife with you?" Rose asked, breaking the silence and easing Thorn's mounting tension.

"No, Liz couldn't make it this time. She had a speaking engagement at the local women's shelter." Bobby looked around, taking Rose's hand in his for a moment. "I'd love to stay and chat some more, but I promised Chuck I'd look him up as soon as I got here. It's great seeing you two again. Later, Thorny Rose."

BOBBY SMILED AND walked off, not realizing the impact he had made on the couple by calling them by their old high school nicknames. However, when Thorn reached to take the hand Bobby had let go of, they both felt a sizzle, and it had nothing to do with the barbeque on the grill.

# — 8 —

ROSE DELIBERATELY TURNED away from
Thorn, pulling her hand from his. She didn't want to
be anywhere near him nor paired with him for any
reason. Her days of being his Rose Petal were long
gone, as well as the relationship they'd shared. He
had dumped her at one of the most critical moments
in her life. When she'd needed him most, he'd desert-
ed her, leaving her to feel the loneliest she'd ever experienced.

It had taken years to get over it. The pain had
gone away in time, along with the aching desire for
him. Gill had made sure she never had time to think
of anyone but him. After a while Rose thought she
had actually forgotten about Thorn and the heartbreak
of her youth. He'd been like a distant memory faded

and maybe not quite real, until yesterday when it all came back at a startling, breakneck speed

Rose realized she had forgotten very little.

Her memories were once again haunting her, with those of Thorn leading the entourage. However, she wasn't that person from high school any longer. She was a changed person. She was stronger and indifferent to Thorn's charm. She wouldn't let the reunion serve as a scenario to reunite them in any way.

Rose searched for Jenny. She finally found her by a grove of trees talking with some other classmates. She didn't know who might have seen her talking with Thorn, and she had no desire to listen to questions from any of them concerning that nightmare that had returned to haunt her. When Jenny waved to her, she gathered her courage and joined her.

"Rose, did you know Helen and her husband are grandparents to triplets? Their daughter, Karen, gave birth four weeks prematurely just two-and-a-half months ago. Their pictures are too cute." Jenny motioned Rose over, holding up the photos.

"Two boys and a girl at one time. What a challenge," Rose murmured. The smiling threesome were in little matching outfits. She'd always wanted a daughter, but the doctor said she was lucky to have the one child she did. She'd endured a difficult delivery, and she couldn't have any more children after that. Too much scar tissue, the doctor had told her. She was grateful for Gill, Jr., but she had always regretted not having a houseful of children.

A car honk was the signal it was time to eat. There were between fifty and sixty people laughing and having a good time as they approached the buffet line. As Jenny and Rose were stepping up to reach for their utensils, Thorn cut directly in front of them. He grabbed three of the extra-sturdy paper plates. Rose and Jenny made no comment but rolled their eyes and followed behind, watching as he filled all three of them.

He smiled as he generously loaded his first plate with potato salad, slaw, macaroni and cheese, and garlic bread. The next plate he piled high with smoked sausage and ribs, along with several slices of brisket. He went to a table and put them down. Then he strolled over to the dessert table and took almost one-fourth of one of the lemon meringue pies Rose had made. He didn't bother even looking at any of the other desserts. Then he went back and sat down.

Rose and Jenny went to a table at the other end of the pavilion and put down their plates. Rose made sure her back was to Thorn. She didn't want to know he was there. She tried to focus on her food, but she kept feeling as if she was being watched. Knowing Thorn was under the same roof was keeping her from enjoying her meal and enjoying time with her friends. It was as if he was there to torture her.

Rose wished she knew why he was doing this. He'd left her, not the other way around. It had taken years to get over being abandoned by him. Now here he was trying to edge himself back into her life.

She was determined, however, to have a good time despite him. After a few more minutes of nibbling at her plate, she accepted she could eat no more of what was before her. Pushing it aside, she stood to go to the dessert table. She had brought a pie, and she wasn't leaving without at least tasting it. As she approached, she heard a deep voice behind her.

"Will you cut me one more piece of pie, Rose Petal?"

Of course, it was Thorn. She recognized his voice as soon as he finished the first word. But before she could comment, Spunky Mulligan, another classmate, suddenly appeared and called, "Smile."

Thorn grabbed Rose around the waist and flashed a big smile. Rose stood in astonishment as the camera clicked. Spunky thanked them and walked off, still taking pictures of the crowd.

"Now about that pie," Thorn repeated.

"Which one did you want?" she shot back, pretending not to know exactly which one he meant.

"Why, yours, of course. The lemon one. You know that's my favorite."

Thorn's honeyed tone took her by surprise. Was he being nice, or was he being sarcastic? In any case, his request was innocent enough. Rose would serve a slice of pie to anyone who asked her.

"S-sure, Thorn. Here you are." Rose served him a large slice, avoiding eye contact. It was difficult enough handing him the slice of pie with his hand brushing against hers. She felt sparks fly at the momentary contact.

Thorn held onto her fingers under the plate until she finally looked up at him. His eyes like black ice peered at her as if he were reading her mind and examining her deepest, most intimate thoughts. The thoughts were the ones she kept trying to push away. They were thoughts about him and her and their tumultuous past. They were the thoughts that she had guarded and kept suppressed all these years that were now trying to surface.

She inhaled a deep breath.

"So, you feel it, too," he said, as he slowly let go of her hand. Thorn then turned and walked back to his table with his slice of lemon meringue pie, leaving a much-shaken Rose.

She paused for a few minutes trying to digest what had just happened. Was he trying to send her a message? She was more bewildered than ever.

With her hands shaking, Rose turned to the dessert table to survey the pies and cakes. She couldn't face anywhere else for the moment. She knew she would look silly just standing there, so she reached to the closest pie she could find. Cutting a fresh slice, she put it on a plate and turned to face the throng of her ex-classmates.

What was Thorn trying to pull by sounding so nice? She knew she couldn't trust him as far as she could throw him. His behavior over the last twenty-four hours had been extremely bizarre, to say the least, not to mention what he just said to her.

Thorn was up to something, but what, Rose didn't have a clue. She was determined to find out before something else happened that she might both dread and regret.

# — 9 —

ROSE LEFT SHORTLY after the barbeque dinner.
The rest of the evening was geared more toward families and their activities. They had set up horseshoes, a
volleyball net, and someone had mentioned softball.
There were large photo albums of different families
being passed around. Some ladies had even brought
scrapbooking materials to work on a fortieth reunion
scrapbook. Everyone seemed to be taking pictures.
Every time someone turned around, someone else
said to smile.

Rose hoped none of the pictures had put her and
Thorn together other than the one at the dessert table.
Jenny stayed and said she would catch a ride. She
wasn't through visiting with all her old friends.

The weather was humid for October. The recent

rain at the airport had only increased the already soaring humidity. Rose's clothes clung to her in an uncomfortable way. She had seen a couple of men looking her direction in a way that annoyed her. She didn't want to be stared at or presumed to be a person who enjoyed that kind of attention. She tried to be a good Christian example for others.

As soon as she arrived home, she immediately prepared for a shower. She couldn't wait to get comfortable. Afterward, she slipped on her coolest cotton gown. Then she settled in front of the family room television. The stress of the day had worn on her, and besides, she hadn't gotten enough sleep the previous two nights due to the scene at the airport. With the soft sound of the TV in the background, it was only a few minutes before Rose was sleeping restfully on the large, overstuffed, cream-colored leather sofa.

She felt like she had just fallen asleep when she heard the doorbell. Jenny had said she would catch a ride with someone, and it was about time for her to return. She pulled on a robe, made her way to the foyer, and slowly opened the door.

"Come in," Rose began, before she noticed her friend wasn't alone. She pulled back to hide behind the door. "I wasn't expecting company, Jenny. I'm not presentable."

JENNY COULD HEAR Thorn whistle softly as he caught sight of Rose. Her hair was disheveled, and the flush of sleep colored her face. She was wearing a cotton gown under her fur-fringed robe. To Thorn, she must be the loveliest creature he'd ever seen. All he could do was stare.

It made Jenny laugh to see how much like high school students they were behaving. They clearly belonged together, even if Rose couldn't see it. The giggle must have finally awakened Rose. As she focused, she realized Jenny's visitor was Thorn, and she gasped and immediately shut the door.

Jenny stood shocked, staring at the exterior side of the closed door.

"Are we welcome or not?" Thorn chuckled.

"I don't know." Jenny looked at him with a smile. "Either way, I'm staying here, and my things are inside. I guess that means I have an invitation, and you're my invited guest. Welcome, Thorn. You may come inside."

Jenny grasped the handle and twisted, relieved Rose had left it unlocked. She pushed it wide and motioned for Thorn to enter.

ROSE RAN TO the sofa and wrapped up in the afghan that had been lying across her. She looked up as Jenny opened the door and motioned Thorn in. Jenny followed on his heels.

"What are you doing here?" Rose questioned grumpily. She could feel his presence in the room. His aura took up all the space.

"Why, darlin', I was just escorting Jenny home. I thought it was only proper to see her to the door. I had no idea you'd already be ready to turn in for the night." Thorn grinned as he spoke.

"What are you talking about? First of all, it's very late; second, I was asleep; and most of all, this is my home, and I can go to bed whenever I want. I didn't invite you in, nor would I have invited you here, regardless, and I would never spend an evening with you." Rose spoke in a huff, still slightly groggy, and irritated at the man's welcome intrusion.

"Now, wait a minute, Rose Petal. I believe you're mistaken." Thorn's good mood clearly wasn't dampened by Rose's boisterous protests. "I distinctly remember spending an evening with you after the Junior-Senior Prom. Don't tell me you don't remember that night—"

Rose interrupted him before he could finish his walk down memory lane. Her voice whipped out in acid-laced rivulets. "Oooh, Thorn. You make me so mad. I don't ever want to think about you and high school or what happened afterward. I've tried my hardest to forget any part of my past that involved you. I'm not the naïve person I was then. I think you need to leave right now!" She was finally wide-awake and growing angrier by the second. She felt her face grow hot.

Thorn just smiled. "Well, all I was doing was trying to set the record straight. Have a good evening, Jenny. You too, Rose Petal."

"You've said enough. You need to leave, Thorn." Rose sat straighter, as she held her afghan around her.

With that, he tipped his hat and walked toward the front door. "Have pleasant dreams, girls. I know I will." He looked at Rose and winked.

She grabbed a throw pillow, aimed it at him, and let it fly. Thorn picked it up, and with an easy motion, he placed it on a nearby chair.

"Now, Rose Petal, don't do something you'll regret tomorrow, like the time you threw the pitcher of tea at me and broke the beautiful cut-glass heirloom your grandmother gave you, not to mention staining the wall." His eyes twinkled with the story. "I helped you clean up the mess you made. If you make a mess tonight, you're on your own."

With a wave, he turned and opened the door. He laughed as he shut it behind him. Rose growled, grabbed a second pillow, and threw it just where he'd been standing.

JENNY TRIED HER best not to laugh. It was truly like a lover's quarrel, except that Rose had emphasized to her several times over the past day that she didn't care about Thorn one iota.

"Oh, that man makes me so mad sometimes. I can hardly stand to be in the same room with him. What gets me is just when he starts acting nice, that's when you know to watch out, because he's about to pull something. I'm glad I have his number. He's not going to pull one over on me. I'll be careful around him, you can rest assured of that. Jenny, you can't trust a Wild Thorn."

As Rose finished, Jenny was relieved her friend's anger appeared to be spent. In Rose's final words, she was certain she heard remorse.

That could mean only one thing: There was still room for hope. Jenny was encouraged, but she couldn't let it show.

# — 10 —

THAT NIGHT WAS even worse. Rose tried to return to the peaceful slumber she'd enjoyed prior to the doorbell ringing. Sleep, however, wasn't her friend. It avoided her at every turn and twist in her bed. For a time, she was too hot. She threw the sheet off, to find she was too cold, and she would reach for it again fifteen minutes later.

Finally, she got up and took a sleeping aid. It was the only way she would get rest that night. Then the dreams manifested themselves: dreams of Thorn and her in high school; and visions of them now, still in love. She could almost feel his warm breath as he kissed her, making her want him even more.

Slowly, she heard something like a faint bell in the distance separating her from her nocturnal lover.

She reached for Thorn as he disappeared, to hear the ringing became louder and louder. Rose wrestled with waking, realizing it was her alarm. She hated those dreams, yet she knew she couldn't control what her mind brought to her at night. She was grateful this night, however, was over, along with the fantasies it had brought with it.

Still, even with the rising sun, Rose didn't feel rested. Her dreams had left her empty and alone. What was worse, her dreams had her longing for Thorn again. That was the part that upset her most, having feelings for someone she knew would only hurt her once more. She had no desire to be with a man who had been so cruel to her in her youth.

"Why must I be tormented and troubled by Thorn?" she mumbled to herself, as she sluggishly climbed from her bed. She didn't want to be a target for his emotional and self-esteem-driven assassinations. She'd barely lived through it once. She didn't think she could survive it again, no matter how much others thought he had changed. Thorn was still Thorn, and she was Rose. He might be the same person from high school, but she'd undergone a transformation. She wasn't the innocent teenage girl to be so easily fooled a second time.

She had become a stronger woman in the past year by being more dependent on God than on people. She could pour her heart out to Him, and He wouldn't judge her or turn her away. She'd discovered He was a God of love and forgiveness. She found great consolation in reading the Psalms and Proverbs from the Bible. It comforted her like no other book had.

She sat at her bedside and read a few passages from God's Word. She drew renewed strength from it. She could face the day and what lay ahead, even if it did involve Thorn.

She felt better as she dressed for the day. Tonight would be her classmates' fortieth reunion banquet held on the top floor of the bank building downtown. It would be an extremely formal event. She'd bought a long dress for the occasion, a soft pearlescent peach affair that was fitted all the way to her hips where it flared ever so slightly. The muted hue blended well with the new color of her nails.

She set out her pearls and her pearl-colored heels on the bed. Everything matched perfectly. She'd get Jenny to help with her make-up. Her friend had done a remarkable job yesterday, from all the compliments she'd received at the barbeque.

Feeling better about the festivities ahead, she headed toward the kitchen, intending to check whether Jenny needed anything. To her surprise, Jenny was already up when she passed by her room. She found her on one of the kitchen barstools with toast and coffee and reading the paper. Rose got the orange juice from the refrigerator.

"Well, good morning, Rose." Jenny looked up with a smile. "I didn't hear you come in."

"I'm sorry. I didn't mean to surprise you. I didn't know you were already up. It's nice to have some help in the kitchen." Rose noticed extra toast and a full pot of coffee.

"It isn't much, but with the day ahead of us, I thought we needed a little something to get us started." Jenny stood. "I haven't gotten out plates. Just you have a seat, and I'll get the table set. I still remember my way around your kitchen, you know." She rifled through a few cabinets, and soon plates and utensils were on the table. She pulled out a couple of glasses and cups, and the drinks were ready.

The two women sat down to the toast, juice, and coffee. Rose always drank hers black, but Jenny had rummaged around and found the cream and sweetener for hers. They were both lost in their thoughts as they began to consume their meal. They turned on the news just in time to catch the daily weather report.

It wasn't good news. The meteorologist predicted microburst showers in the area, off and on until sometime tomorrow afternoon.

Jenny frowned. "I really didn't want to have to worry about my evening being marred by rain. Oh, my." She picked up a slice of toast and bit off the corner, as she looked out the window at the building clouds.

The last thing Rose needed was an impending storm added to the already volatile situation between her and Thorn coming up this evening. They could produce sparks in the wettest of seasons. It didn't matter what was in the atmosphere, them coming together could produce a blazing inferno.

With the dark, ominous clouds brewing, who knew what would happen before the reunion was over?

# — 11 —

THORN WOKE UP on the wrong side of the bed, just like he did almost every day. He never seemed to wake to the thought that the day would be a great one. His life was a rut and he knew what a rut was.

"A rut's nothing but a grave with the ends kicked out," he groaned to himself, as he crawled out of bed to make himself some coffee.

He'd never been the same after the break-up with Rose. Even though it was forty years ago, he still felt the loss. Sure, he went through the motions of being alive. He got up, showered, and went to work. He came home, watched a little TV, ate some dinner, and then usually slept.

One of the things he was grateful for was his job. It was hard and demanding outside work. It kept him tired and often exhausted. Even though he was a supervisor, he didn't stay in the office. He went out in the field and checked on his workers every day. He often had to help make sure the job was done right. Too many kids these days didn't seem to care or take pride in their work. Thorn felt he had to be there to watch for careless but costly mistakes.

Today would be different. He was going to his high school's fortieth reunion. The love of his life would be there.

He smiled as he thought about her, but just as quickly, his smiled paled as he considered his plan. What if it didn't work? What would he do then? Could he walk out on Rose, knowing they might've had a go at a second chance? Would he be able to cut her out of his life forever?

His thoughts plagued him as he drank his morning coffee and worried about the evening ahead. It was so easy to plan with Rose at a distance, nothing more than a memory or slight distraction in his day. But now that he'd seen her and kissed her, he didn't know if he could go through with the plan he'd so carefully devised.

He'd thought he wanted to hurt Rose, crush her spirit, and leave her the way she'd left him. Now he had different feelings about her. Seeing how vulnerable she was made him feel like he needed to protect her, but from whom?

With slow, insightful trepidation, he came to the realization that he needed to protect her from himself.

All he was ever going to do was hurt her. Yet now, at this moment, that was the last thing he wanted to do to his Rose Petal.

A part of him still loved her. He thought he'd finally killed out any tender feelings he had for her. He thought the ache in his heart had finally stopped. Somewhere, deep in the recesses of his soul, there was a part of him that had never stopped loving her, and that was the part tormenting him. That was the part that had made him grab her with reckless abandon in the airport terminal and kiss her.

That one tiny part of his heart had never let go of her. Now here it was bigger and stronger than ever, and it still wanted Rose. It was more than a want. It was a need. He needed Rose, despite what she had done to him; he still needed her, and now maybe more than ever. He was filled with desire for her; he wanted to know her every thought, feeling, and sentiment about every little thing.

That was a dangerous place for his heart to be.

It wasn't the plan he'd so carefully mapped out. He'd have to see his original plan through or end up in a bigger mess than he was already in. His one true love would learn to understand the old saying that all's fair in love and war. He was ready for the war, because he knew he couldn't handle the love. He had already tried that route. Rose would probably just rip him apart like she did the last time. If she did, there was no distant battlefield to escape to.

He also had someone else to think about now,

someone he could never hurt no matter what happened to him. He would have to keep on his pre-planned path, even if it meant losing all hope of being with Rose forever. He didn't have a choice.

Sometimes life was cruel like that. People didn't get to pick the choices they would like. They were stuck with the hand fate dealt them, or at least that was what Thorn thought. And he was tired of trying and getting nowhere. Yes, it was all about to change, and it had nothing to do with the hand of fate.

# — 12 —

ROSE HAD DONE some thinking of her own.

Nothing Thorn was doing was what she'd expected, based on their last meeting and the lecture she'd received from his parents. She'd never forgotten that horrible day nearly forty years ago. It was a day she'd tried hard to erase from her mind, but it came back occasionally to haunt her in her dreams, asleep or awake.

When he'd walked out on her, and his parents had told her he didn't love her and never had, the truth had consumed her with its finality: He'd only married her out of duty's sake. They said he didn't even want to tell her good-bye.

Then when he came into the room where she was and tried to kiss her, she'd said she would see him in his grave first. Those had been bitter words from a young girl with a broken heart, a girl who had just watched her life's dreams evaporate before her eyes. Her hopes had been cruelly vanquished, with no hope of restoration. Thorn's parents had assured her of that.

She'd been so hurt by what they told her that she didn't want to speak with him ever again. However, that had been youth and rash behavior speaking. She knew she wouldn't respond that way now. She'd changed a lot over the years. She'd been married to Gill for nearly four decades, and she'd raised a wonderful son. Then, there was her newfound faith in Christ. Rose knew she'd matured and would have handled the situation very differently, if she'd felt then what she did now. At times like this, she wished she could have been born old. Then, her choices from so long ago would have been the better ones she now knew how to make.

"Penny for your thoughts."

The words jarred Rose back to reality. "What? Oh, I'm sorry. Jenny, were you saying something?" Rose realized she'd been distracted, and the silence in the room must have been obvious.

"You were so deep in thought, and it seemed so serious, that I didn't want to interrupt you, but I thought we might need to map out our plan for the day." Jenny smiled. "You didn't even hear your name the first time I spoke it. Where were you?"

Rose didn't answer her question, instead pausing until Jenny reached and touched her arm. Then, with a smile, she forced herself to go on. "A plan. We do need to map one out, don't we? I'll need to get ready. I want you to do my make-up again, if you have the time. Everyone loved the way I looked yesterday afternoon, so maybe a repeat performance would be nice."

Rose had been very brusque the day before, and she wanted to make it up to Jenny. Besides, she really thought her friend had outdone herself, at least if Rose judged by the compliments she'd received.

"Repeat performance, nothing." Jenny winked at her. "We'll go for an even more exciting look." She stood and pulled Rose from her seat. "It's the evening, and everyone will look more glamorous. We'll show them what you've really got. Let's start by putting a few curlers in your hair in random directions, so your hair will stand out when it falls in wisps down your neck." She giggled and began lifting Rose's hair just to see what the effect might look like.

Jenny sounded truly excited about giving Rose a makeover again. Rose was relieved her friend didn't hold a grudge. Jenny had always been that way, forgiving and letting anger and disappointments go. She always seemed focused on the future and the next adventure coming her way.

Rose sighed. She wished she could be more like that. However, she always took things seriously and never backed down once her mind was made up. She had a difficult time apologizing, and she wanted to blame most of her faults on others. Even now that she was truly a Christian, it was a laborious effort to admit she was wrong.

Seeing the excitement in Jenny's eyes as she planned her makeover, Rose felt guilty. Jenny had asked her a question last year that had made Rose angry, and she hadn't spoken to her in the intervening months. If Jenny hadn't reached out to her, she might have lost her friend forever. It embarrassed and saddened Rose to think she had treated her friend that way.

"Hm, Jenny?" Rose felt her words stumble. She wanted to apologize, and she was finding it very challenging.

"Yes?" Jenny was gathering her hair supplies, and she paused to give Rose her attention.

"I just, well, I just wanted to say I'm sorry about the misunderstanding we had back at Thanksgiving last year. I've always thought of you as a true friend and still do. Can, can you forgive me?" Rose finished in a halting tone, and she looked away, not sure of Jenny's response.

"But, of course, I forgive you," Jenny replied warmly, as she gave Rose a hug to reassure her there were no hard feelings.

As Rose felt relief course through her, she hugged Jenny back, and she felt a few tears at the corners of her eyes, revealing even more of her emotions.

"I'm not letting a little confusion wreck our forty-five-year relationship. It'll take more than that to make me stay angry at you," Jenny continued.

Rose smiled. At least she had one friend she could trust and count on. Maybe she'd be able to get through this last part of the reunion after all. Thorn didn't have to ruin it for her. She could stay close to her valued companion and trusted friend. She looked up to see Jenny motioning her to a kitchen chair.

"Let's see. I have a spray bottle here somewhere. We must wet each strand of hair as it gets rolled. That'll make it hold its shape."

Rose smiled as Jenny busied herself making her beautiful. It was good to be fussed over, no matter the results this makeover incurred, and Rose was content to let Jenny be the one to do it.

# — 13 —

BITTERNESS LIKE GALL ate at Anna Wilder-McQueen. She had thought this would be a good idea, but now that she was here to confront her birth mother, she wasn't so sure.

She gazed at herself critically in the mirror. Tonight, she wore a soft peach dress with pearl sequins on the bodice. The top was fitted with a scooped neck. The dress tumbled in loose folds from the waist down. She was tall like her father, standing nearly six feet, but that was where the similarities stopped. She didn't favor her father or her grandparents. She'd never seen a picture of her mother, but she knew she must favor her by the remarks her father occasionally made about her eyes or complexion, though his comments were usually whispered under his breath and not meant for her to hear.

Memories of things her grandparents had told her had started to surface since arriving in town, causing the hurt and angry emotions of her childhood to resonate in overwhelming feelings of rejection and abandonment; and the idea of facing someone who had never wanted her to begin with was a hard pill to swallow.

Yet, she needed to show the world she'd overcome those emotions, and she needed people to see how well she'd done, despite not being loved or wanted by that woman. She had graduated valedictorian of her senior class and had finished her bachelor's and master's degrees in physical therapy before going on and pursuing her doctorate. She now worked for a very prestigious sports therapy company. The love and concern she'd been raised with had been enough. Her *grandparents* had been enough. She'd demonstrated to the world she hadn't needed what everyone said she must have to survive: a mother's love.

Now she intended to prove to the woman who'd cast her aside that she'd never needed her to begin with. Tonight, once and for all, she intended to prove to herself and the world, but most importantly to the woman who gave her birth, that she had succeeded. The woman who had given her away and never looked back would know. The woman who had never given her a chance, but who had simply turned her head and walked out on her while she was only seconds old, would see a successful Anna.

She'd been told the story repeatedly as a child when she questioned her grandparents or her father about her mother. Her father usually didn't say much, telling her, "She didn't love either of us, Anna." Then a somber expression would edge across his face, and he would be lost in thought.

Her grandparents, however, were always quick to explain just how much her mother didn't love her and how fortunate she was to have loving grandparents who did. She'd been raised by them in the early years of her life, interspersed with brief stints spent alone with her father. He was usually off somewhere on some job, out of the state or out of the country.

It wasn't until she was fourteen and her grandparents were both tragically killed in a car accident that her father was forced to care for her full time. Anna had been in the car with them, but thankfully she'd been protected in the back seat of the large luxury vehicle, when a moving van suffered a blowout and swerved into oncoming traffic, hitting their car head on. Both of her grandparents died instantly.

Anna underwent physical therapy for several months while her broken legs and fractured hip healed. It was a slow and painful process. Despite that, she made a full recovery with no permanent damage to either her legs or hip, doing well enough to play basketball her junior and senior years of high school. Her experience from the wreck was what prompted her to become a physical therapist.

Her father turned out to be a very loving and patient man. He quit his military career, and he took a civilian job, so he could be home with her. Anna realized he'd made a sacrifice in his lifestyle to do that, but she never heard him complain about it. He always made her feel special, like she was the most important person in his world. That was why she'd agreed to come to this activity with him. She wanted in some small way to show him the gratitude she felt because he had been so selfless and altruistic.

Her thoughts continued to ramble as she began to get dressed for the evening, and she dressed and re-dressed, adjusting her outfit's tasteful accoutrements over and over to occupy her time. She had purchased some pearl-hued sandals and a matching handbag. Her father had given her a long, beautiful strand of pearls he brought back from Thailand. She had packed them carefully and wanted to wear them, so her father would know how much she treasured the personal gifts he lavished on her.

# — 14 —

JENNY WAS FINISHING Rose's make-up, telling her friend that her hair had turned out adorable. It made her look ten years younger. With the darker make-up for the evening, she looked even more attractive than she had the day before at the picnic.

Jenny laughed and held up a mirror. "No one will be able to take their eyes off you. Your hair and make-up look fabulous on you. Let's see how the dress does."

Jenny was doing her best to encourage Rose. She had to. Rose had been hesitant about her hair and make-up, saying it was too heavy. In the mirror, though, Jenny was sure Rose could see her smoky gray eyes as they twinkled, bringing out depths of color that were normally not visible with the make-up she usually wore.

Jenny also pointed out how Rose's dress complemented her soft complexion, contrasting with the rich shade of her hair, with its soft chestnut brown color set off with a few darker auburn red highlights scattered throughout. Her hair made the dress look even more muted and subdued.

When Rose stood, her dress cascaded to the floor, revealing only the toes of her shoes. The fitted peach gossamer gown made Rose look ethereal. She had a fairy-like quality, being so petite, with a fluttering layer of the sheer, sequined gown hanging loosely over the satin underneath.

Jenny was very pleased with the final product she'd brought out in Rose. Now she had to work on herself. She'd bought a stretchy, black, slinky dress whose fabric had a satin-like sheen. It hung to the middle of her calf. She added a hairpiece and pulled her own hair up and under it, letting a few tendrils hang loose in the back and around the edges. She clipped on oversized black faux-diamond-accented jewelry. Her heels were black with large, chunky faux diamonds across the toes over black pantyhose. When she finished her make-up, she'd transformed herself, as well.

Both women would stand out in the crowd this evening, despite the efforts of others who might try to outdo them.

Jenny finished her final layer of lipstick just as the doorbell rang.

"I've got it, Jenny!" Rose called to her friend.

"It's probably Roxanne and Jack. Tell them I'm about ready."

Jenny smiled, certain Roxanne and Jack would be caught off-guard. She entered the living room just in time to see them walking around Rose, unable to get enough of how beautiful she looked. Then, Jenny stepped into the room, making her entrance, and taking the two visitors aback once again.

"Girl, you've turned up the heat in your all-black style." Roxanne giggled and prodded Jack with her elbow.

After the first glance, Jack had the good sense to not even look, and with a deep breath, he asked if they were ready to go. Even though they were a few minutes early, everyone seemed anxious to get the night started. Rose grabbed her purse, set the alarm, locked the door, and walked outside with everyone else in tow. She told Jack and Roxanne how pleased she was to have the opportunity to ride in the new Lincoln they'd bought only a few weeks before.

Jenny walked up to the car, reaching out to touch a piece of chrome. "I feel like a rock star tonight." She raised her arms in the air as if waving to adoring fans. The other three laughed, and Rose reached to pull her arms down.

Rose turned to Jack, "Seriously, this will make for a great time this evening. It's nice being chauffeured, even if Jenny does feel more like a rock star than someone attending her forty-year reunion. Thank you again for offering to drive. It takes a lot of stress off me."

"Happy to do so. Besides," Jack laughed lightly, "I enjoy escorting beautiful women into the city."

"Oh, you do, do you?" Roxanne popped out, causing everyone to laugh. She gave him a playful pinch before she crossed her arms and glared at him.

DURING THE RIDE to the reunion, the three women laughed and regaled each other with stories they'd learned about their ex-classmates at the barbeque the day before. Jack just listened, grabbing an occasional glance in the rear-view mirror of the two women he and Roxanne had picked up. Roxanne only pinched him one more time, though, as he was very careful to glance when she wasn't watching, and the trip ended without incident.

When they arrived, the line of cars to be parked moved quickly. At the door, the three beautiful women and their escort stepped from the interior of the car and into the soft glow of the bank tower's lighted parking garage's porte-cochere. The valet smiled at his chance to take the keys to Jack's new Lincoln, and the four walked inside the bank's glass elevator.

Jack escorted Roxanne while Jenny and Rose walked together to the elevator. Once they stepped inside, Jack pushed the twenty-first floor button. With a soft surge, the elevator made its way to the top floor of the bank tower, with the numbers on the readout clicking swiftly through their proscribed pattern.

As the group stepped from the door, they were bathed in soft candlelight. The overall view was breathtaking. The room had an elegance reminiscent of a bygone era with large chandeliers, lots of crystal, silver, china, and huge palms and ferns.

THE GROUP SIGNED in, put on nametags, and looked for their table number. They were sitting together, along with four more people from their class. Fortunately, Jenny had been on the planning committee and had put Thorn and his guest as far as they could be at the other end of the ballroom. There were only a few people at their end, so Rose was able to relax and focus on the events ahead and not on Thorn. At least that was what she hoped to do.

Everyone ordered drinks, and several appetizers were served, while guests mingled and waited for the dinner to be brought out. Rose quietly sipped her beverage, and then Jenny whispered, "I see Thorn, and I think he's headed this way."

"I believe I'll go powder my nose." Rose got up and headed to the ladies' room. Once in the safety of the private space, she let out a deep breath. She'd been holding it, afraid she would hear her name being yelled from across the banquet room like at the airport. She glanced around and noticed a couple of other classmates touching up their make-up and talking on their cellphones. She spoke and visited with them for a minute or two before they left to go back to their tables.

Finally, after about ten minutes, Rose decided she would head back to her table as well. She wouldn't let Thorn ruin her night. She had a right to be here as much as he did. Things would be fine if he kept his distance.

With new resolve, Rose started for her table and the shock of her life.

# — 15 —

AS SOON AS Rose arrived back at her table, she knew something was amiss. The expression on Jenny's face was one of total bewilderment. Roxanne's was more akin to confusion, bordering on horror.

"What's the matter? What happened while I was gone?" Rose questioned, looking curiously from Jenny to Roxanne.

Jenny spoke up with hesitation in her voice, "Is there anything you want to tell us about you and Thorn, anything, perhaps, that you've never revealed?" She spoke slowly, making sure Rose got her question.

Rose frowned. She was already aware Thorn was present, and that was bad enough. Now her friends were acting strangely, and they were asking questions on a topic she wanted to put as far from her as possible. She brushed off the question with a pert reply, "Not really. He's in the past, and that's where I want to keep him."

Roxanne leaned in closely, staring intently at her friend. "You mean nothing happened between him and you that you want to share with us? Maybe, like, you know, something important? It seems there were a few months just after graduation that were unaccounted for. In fact, if I remember correctly, there was almost a year you and Thorn were out of touch with everyone."

Rose took a deep breath and replied as civilly as possible, "No, nothing I can think of that would matter now. That was a long time ago, and it was just a year better forgotten."

She had no intention of discussing it with them. It didn't matter now, anyway.

"Even if you don't think it's important now, can you think of something in your past that Thorn might bring up, something that might surprise us?"

Jenny's question dug a little closer to home, and Rose began to squirm. It was as though her friend had to ferret out some truth from Rose, when she didn't know what they expected her to say.

Rose looked at their faces, realizing they were almost ashen in color. What could Thorn have said or done that would make them react like this?

Rose thought for a minute and then sighed, "Well, for about seven months, right after high school, Thorn and I were married. But—"

"And then what happened?" blurted Roxanne, before Rose had a chance to finish.

"Nothing," Rose replied. "He dumped me and went off to find himself a war. I've not seen him since, not until this weekend. That's why I never mentioned it before. We were together for such a short time, and then he and his family moved away. We never spoke again until the other night in the airport, when he welcomed me to a weekend of torture."

Rose could tell by the expressions on her friends' faces she hadn't answered their questions. In fact, they looked more puzzled than ever.

"You mean you were married, and nothing else happened during that time that you want to share with us, something that we believe could be important?"

Roxanne kept questioning her, and Rose wondered where this could all be leading. By this time, she was a little aggravated at the questioning. She had just shared the most secret part of her life. Even Gill, Jr. didn't know she had been married before. Now her friends were acting like she had some big secret to share. She didn't appreciate being interrogated by them about something Thorn had obviously contrived to make her look bad. She was determined not to let him ruin her evening.

"Where's Thorn?" she questioned Jenny. "I'm getting to the bottom of whatever it is he's accused me of." Rose stood and looked out over the ballroom. About a hundred people were scattered throughout the space.

Jenny jumped up, too.

"I'll help you find him, Rose." She took Rose's arm and began aiming her toward the other end of the banquet hall. They had only taken about twenty steps or so when Jenny whispered, "Rose, I see him. He's straight ahead."

As Rose stepped forward, it was as if the crowd parted and let her and Jenny through. People were staring and whispering, some in shocked surprise, others almost laughing.

Rose was becoming more upset by the minute, and she intended to set the record straight.

THORN HAD BEEN visiting with some of his classmates when he noticed the pair approaching out of the corner of his eye. He slowly turned toward Rose, gaping at her, speechless.

The most beautiful vision of loveliness he could imagine was standing only a few feet from him, and it was his Rose Petal. She was coming toward him; the most stunning creature in the world was walking up to him.

He flashed a huge smile. It was then he realized she wasn't smiling.

In fact, she looked irate or worse.

Rose glanced at those standing around Thorn, and she motioned for him to bend down so she could whisper in his ear. Just as he started to lean toward her, a woman approached him. Thorn turned his head to her, and Rose's eyes followed.

It was then Rose's legs buckled, and Jenny grabbed her just before she went to her knees.

# — 16 —

ROSE DIDN'T FAINT, but she felt very close. In front of her stood a near replica of her, all the way down to the peach-colored dress Rose wore. The woman sported a similar color gown, merely a shade darker, which brought out the deep highlights in her hair. Around her neck, she boasted a long strand of pearls to match those sewn on Rose's dress. The only noticeable difference was Thorn's wavy auburn hair and his height.

Her face, however, was Rose's.

She had Rose's creamy complexion and high cheekbones. The shape of her cloudy blue eyes and delicate mouth could be from no one other than Rose. Her slim neckline mirrored Rose's as well.

Rose stared at her in shocked surprise, stunned

into complete silence. The woman also seemed to be taken aback by Rose's appearance, seeing a diminutive mirror of her own face. She simply gawked at Rose, as Thorn looked from one to the other. He seemed pleased at how they favored.

"Well, at last they meet. Rose Petal, I'd like to introduce you to our daughter, Anna. Anna, this is your mother, Rosemary, better known as Rose Petal." Thorn spoke just loudly enough for the two women to hear.

All the air went out of Rose. She couldn't breathe, and she felt herself starting to fall. She was helpless to control it. The next thing she knew, strong hands were lifting her and reassuring her everything was going to be okay. It was as if she were having one of her unexplainable dreams. Only now it was real.

A few seconds later, Rose was reclining on a gold brocade couch with a glass of water being pressed to her lips. Then she heard voices.

"Come on, Rose Petal. Drink this."

Another asked, "Should we call a doctor?"

Rose opened her eyes. It wasn't a dream. There was Thorn sitting beside her and offering her sips of water, while Jenny patted her hand. Things were slowly coming into focus. But where was the other woman? Then she looked beyond Thorn and saw her with eyes blazing. The creature who looked so much like Rose lashed out at her.

"Is this the little act you put on to get my Daddy's attention? Well, it might work for him, but it certainly doesn't work for me," Anna spat venomously.

"Wait, I'm confused." Rose tried to pull herself up, and she paused as she thought about what Thorn had said to her before she blacked out. The memory of his words crystalized in her mind, and she rasped out her words. "What do you mean, our daughter? We never had any children, Thorn. Not any that lived. The only baby I gave birth to that lived was Gill, Jr."

Wrapped in the overwhelming revelation washing over her, Rose could see only Thorn and the unknown woman he'd claimed to be her daughter. She was blinded to the people around her by this sudden turn of events, and she threw harsh words at him.

"The child you and I had was stillborn. Your mother told me that when she came into the hospital room. She said it was born dead. She didn't even tell me if it was a boy or a girl."

Rose glared as she realized everyone in the room now knew their shared history, all the while moving her eyes between Thorn and the strange woman that looked so much like her.

"Well, I'm very much alive, with little thanks to you, mommy dearest." Anna stepped forward, her voice a biting tirade against Rose's angry defense. "You don't have to continue to put on this dramatic scene, when you very well knew I lived. My grandmother told me how you wouldn't even look at me when I was born, and you said you wanted nothing to do with my father or me. She said you were sorry you'd ever met my father. So, don't go and try to change the story now!"

Anna was almost shouting in Rose's face. Other guests were starting to gather around, and Rose could only watch the face that was so much like hers.

JENNY, WHO KNEW Rose well, could tell by her expression this was all new information to her. Rose seemed almost in a state of shock. Thorn was watching her, and from his expression, he was beginning to have growing doubts himself.

She stepped to her friend, and she took her hand to comfort her.

THORN HAD NEVER actually questioned Rose back then. He'd taken his parents' word that she'd said all those hurtful things. In fact, they had insisted that he not even go in to say good-bye. They said she didn't want to speak with him, and he needed to let her have her way.

They had repeated themselves more than once and forbade it explicitly.

Thorn couldn't let her go that easily, not his wife, not the woman he loved. He was distraught at the idea she wouldn't want to see him. There had been no suggestion before the baby's birth that she felt this way.

When his parents went to sign the papers, he snuck in Rose's hospital room. That was when she said she'd see him burn before she ever kissed him again.

She was angry that day; he'd had no trouble telling that. Rose had never been much of an actor. She wore her feelings on her face, and her body language was usually easy to read.

Right now, Rose was stiff, and her pallor revealed that she was alarmed and even fearful. After a few minutes, she spoke in a labored tone.

"Thorn, this is the cruelest joke I've ever known anyone to pull. To find some woman who resembles me to help you carry this out is even more malicious and spiteful. That you would use our precious baby, something I'd wanted more than anything in this world, and turn it into some kind of twisted, hurtful comedy is even beyond what I ever thought you were capable of."

As soon as she finished speaking, Rose turned to Jenny. "Please help me to my feet. I believe I've had all of this reunion and all of Thorn I can stand."

Anna spat at her, "Oh, make a big scene and then exit. How very theatrical of you."

She was quickly interrupted by Thorn.

"Anna, leave Rose Petal alone. She doesn't need this right now."

Anna pressed her lips together and crossed her arms, not happy about this situation at all.

Thorn could see the pain and suffering on Rose's face. Something was wrong. This scenario wasn't going as planned. Rose hadn't been embarrassed by his divulging her secret. She was hurt and angry, and more than anything, she appeared surprised.

Rose turned to him and spoke through gritted teeth. "Don't ever speak to me again, Thorn Wilder. As long as you live, I never want to hear from you or see you again. You've hurt me for the very last time. I never want any dealings to do with you, ever! If you were trying to embarrass me, you've succeeded. If you were trying to make me despise you, well, you've accomplished that goal, as well."

WITH HER LAST remark, Rose stood and walked to her table to retrieve her purse and leave. She told Jack and Roxanne she would catch a taxi home. Jenny offered to accompany her, but she said she needed to be alone. She never looked back. She didn't stop to see the expression of utter and complete devastation creeping across Thorn's broken features.

# — 17 —

THE REUNION CROWD was abuzz after Rose left. Not everyone knew what had happened, but everybody had watched Rose leave, and most of them saw Thorn's face afterward. They could tell his daughter seemed to be a big part of this puzzling night as well.

Only minutes after Rose left, Thorn and Anna made their departure as well, leaving onlookers more perplexed than ever. Jenny, however, went back to her assigned table. She sat down stoically and just stared at the food placed in front of her. What had been revealed tonight would change lives forever.

Jenny just couldn't figure this out. Rumors were all she'd known of Thorn and Rose and that missing year. None of them had ever been substantiated, though. Apparently, from her face tonight, poor Rose didn't seem to have a clue what was going on.

Thorn had started out the evening so smugly, but he had seemed tormented in the end. Then there was his daughter, rather, their daughter, who had been a secret all these years. How could Rose not know the baby had lived? His parents couldn't have kept that from her no matter how much they wanted to. The doctor would have told her at delivery.

Yet, Rose had never mentioned a doctor. Surely there had to have been a doctor who delivered the baby. He would have told Rose the truth.

Roxanne interrupted her thoughts.

"What happened back there, Jenny? It was like World War Three was about to start. And the woman Thorn introduced as his daughter, how is she involved? I thought Rose only has the one son."

"So did Rose, until now," explained Jenny. She told everyone at the table about the incident and Rose's reaction. No one could believe it. The story sounded like something you'd see on television, not reality played out right before their eyes.

"Poor Rose. So she never knew she had a child by him? How can someone not know something like that?" Barker Sampley, a guest seated at the table, asked the question. Jenny recounted Rose's conversation and Thorn's earlier comments about how big Anna had been when she was born.

"Rose was put to sleep for a caesarian section because the baby was so big; you know how small Rose is compared to Thorn. But it was too late. The baby was already coming, and it delivered the normal way.

"When she awakened, only Thorn's mother was in the room. She told Rose the baby was born dead. At least that's what I understand, from what Rose just told Thorn."

Jenny put her hand over her mouth, still dazed by it all. After that, she just picked at her food. She had no appetite and couldn't enjoy herself knowing her best friend had just received such shocking news.

She excused herself and went to the ladies' room to call Rose on her cell. When Rose didn't pick up, Jenny became alarmed. Back at the table, she shared her concerns with Roxanne and excused herself for the evening, explaining that she was going to Rose's. She would help Rose uncover the truth once and for all about Thorn.

Jenny phoned for a taxi and headed down the elevator for the ground floor. What a night this fortieth reunion had turned out to be!

Her ride was waiting when she reached the lower level. She gave directions and thought about the evening's events, while he drove into the night. The vehicle had only reached the outskirts of the city when her phone rang. She breathed a sigh of relief, certain Rose was returning her call. She tapped the answer icon and spoke with emotion into the device.

"Rose, I was so worried when you didn't answer your phone a few minutes ago. Are you okay? I should have gone with you, but you said you didn't want company right then, and you'd see me later. But then when you didn't answer, I got worried. I'm on my way over."

There was silence, and then a low, guttural, broken voice spoke, "This isn't Rose. It's Thorn."

Now it was Jenny's turn for all the breath to leave her body. Why was Thorn calling her?

# — 18 —

"WE NEED TO talk before you get to Rose's. I'm really messed up right now. I've got to unload all this on someone. Can you meet me somewhere?"

Thorn's voice came out in ragged bits edged with panic, not his usual liquid, smooth tone. Jenny thought for just a second before responding. He sounded desperate, and that frightened her. In her mind, Thorn wasn't afraid of anything or anybody.

"Yes, sure. I'll meet you. Where?"

"How about that all-night truck stop on the Interstate? The restaurant is open, and I'll buy us both a cup of coffee."

"Okay. I'll see you there in about ten minutes," Jenny replied, and the phone went dead in her hand. She looked at it, certain of how devastated Thorn must be to not even say good-bye.

Jenny's taxi pulled to the front door of the Double Clover Twenty-Four Hour Restaurant. Thorn was waiting and paid her cab fare. He also gave the driver a substantial tip. Jenny thanked him as he escorted her in and led her toward a back booth where it was quieter and less crowded.

The waitress came by and took their order for some coffee and toast. She tried to flirt with Thorn, and she was disappointed when he ignored her completely. Thorn just stared ahead glassy-eyed, like Jenny wasn't even there. He seemed to be in his own world.

Finally, he spoke.

"Jenny, I have a bad feeling about tonight, like I really blew it," he started. "I have a sense that Rose didn't even know she had a daughter."

He paused for a moment, glancing Jenny's way for an instant, then as quickly looking away. His face twisted as he tried to regain his self-control.

"Hmm," Jenny murmured, not sure what to say.

"But I know that's impossible. What do you know about Rose and me after high school? What's she told you?"

Jenny waited for a minute while the waitress poured their coffee and set down their toast.

"Well, I do know the rumors that you two were married for a short while during that year after high school, although Rose never talks about it and has sworn me to secrecy with what little she's told me; I don't think even Gill, Jr. knows his mom might have been married before. She called me right after you broke up with her and left. She was so distraught I'm certain she doesn't even remember doing that. By the time I could get home from college to console her, her parents had been relocated to Germany. They were stationed there for the next several years."

ALL THORN HEARD was that he had broken up with Rose. The words twisted in him: *She called me right after you broke up with her and left.*

"Wait, hold on a second." Thorn's eyes pleaded with Jenny, hoping for her to correct her story. He didn't even hear the last of the conversation. His brain was locked on *you broke up with her.* "Did you just say that I was the one that broke up with her?"

"Yes, Rose has always said you broke up with her when she needed you most." Jenny's eyes let him know it was the truth.

Thorn felt like he'd been sucker-punched. He stared into his coffee cup for what seemed like eons. Slowly, he raised his head.

"Jenny, I want you to hear the truth from me, exactly as I remember it. Don't interrupt me, just listen. We can talk about discrepancies afterward. Right now, I just want to talk."

Just as he began, his cell phone rang. He glanced at the number as he answered it.

"Hi, Sugar. No, I'm fine, really. I just needed a cup of coffee, that's all. I've run into a friend here, so

I may visit for a while. Head on to bed. I've got my room key. Don't wait up. We've both got a plane to catch tomorrow. Love you, too, Anna. Bye."

He looked at Jenny sheepishly. "Daughters can be so over-protective, sometimes."

"So can wives and girlfriends," Jenny nodded, as she replied with a dry twist to her words.

# — 19 —

THORN BEGAN, "MY folks never did approve of
Rose Petal. They considered her family poor white
trash, because during the time they were both stationed in Killeen, her father was only a sergeant and
my father was a general. They accused my sweet
Rose Petal of trying to get her dad a promotion by
using my father's influence. Not once in our entire
relationship did she even mention her father's rank to
me. But my parents brought it up every time I turned
around.

"Rose Petal and I had been going out since our
junior year. Her parents were strict on her, and we
dated very little. We'd only shared a few innocent
kisses. Finally, the senior prom came around, and her
parents agreed she could stay out until 1:00 a.m. We

ditched the prom about 11:00 and took my parents' big new Cadillac and went parking out at the lake.

"We'd never made out like that. She was like a drug to me. I couldn't resist her. The more I had of her, the more I wanted. I couldn't stop once we got started. It was only that one night, but that's all it took.

"She didn't tell me until she knew for sure, a month or so later. Her father came over to my parents' house ready to kill me. Of course, my parents accused her of seducing me, which wasn't true.

"In the end, we married and moved into an efficiency apartment. It didn't seem to matter to Rose. She was always happy and kept the place spotless.

"I was so in love with her, I didn't see any faults in her, but my parents sure did. They were constantly saying things like she wasn't a very good cook, or she slept a lot. She was pregnant; of course, she slept a lot. She didn't cook because the smell of food made her nauseous. But the few times she did cook, her food was always fabulous. I didn't care. I loved Rose, and she seemed to love me.

"Then my parents came by one time while I wasn't home, and some guy was at our house. That's when they began to accuse her of cheating on me. Then I became divided between believing her or my parents.

"Later, I found out it was your brother bringing a letter from you at college. But by then, seeds of jealousy were rooted in my heart. I'd call her during the day, or check to see if she'd really gone to the laundromat, anything, just to keep tabs on her. My parents were making me crazy.

"Finally, when Rose was so big she could hardly move, they started telling me she was lazy. Rose was having a difficult time even walking. Anna was born almost three weeks premature, due to her size; she weighed ten pounds and four ounces. She was to be delivered caesarian at the last minute, but the baby had already started down the birth canal.

"It was a very scary time. Rose Petal almost died. Of course, my folks were right there to accuse her of being pregnant by someone else, and that was why the baby was early. The doctors had put Rose to sleep because of the pain she was in. Her parents weren't there because my folks refused to call them and let them know until after the baby was born and we'd left the hospital.

"After the doctor delivered Anna, my parents came out of the hospital room and said Rose didn't love me. They said she was angry because the baby had ruined her figure. They said she never wanted to see me again, and she didn't want the baby, either.

"I was so crushed I didn't know what to think. The happiest day of my life had just exploded in my face. I knew we had a few problems, but I loved Rose Petal with all my heart.

"My parents assured me they would adopt the baby and raise it. They also said Rose's last wish was that she never see me again. My parents then went in another room to sign some paperwork.

"I couldn't help myself. I had to see her just one last time to try to convince her to stay with me and not leave. I thought if I could just talk to her or kiss her, I could persuade her to stay. But when I went into the room, it was already too late. She looked at me with such disgust and hatred that I knew it was over.

"But I was still determined to try. I wanted to kiss her good-bye, but she made it clear I was one match away from a bonfire if I touched her. That was the last time I saw her. She completed all the divorce proceedings through my parents. I was already scheduled to ship out by then, and I didn't care if I lived or died.

"My heart was so broken by Rose Petal's rejection of me and our daughter, I had no will to live. It was only the mercy of God that kept me alive and brought me home. He knew my little Rose would need me later in life."

Thorn stopped and took a sip of coffee.

JENNY SAT TOTALLY blindsided. This wasn't the story she'd heard from Rose. She had only uncovered Thorn and Rose's turbulent break-up in bits and pieces over the years, and it didn't match what Thorn had just relayed to her.

Now Jenny didn't know what to believe.

# — 20 —

"WELL, DO YOU have anything to say?" Thorn finally asked Jenny after several minutes of quiet.

"What? Oh, sorry, I was just trying to digest everything. Your version of the break-up doesn't match what Rose has told me, which isn't all that much, but I'm sure this isn't what she believes happened."

Jenny looked at her hands and fiddled with a ring she was wearing, and then she reached for her coffee. She was at a loss what to say, and she needed time to come to grips with Thorn's version of events. Just then Thorn's hand reached for hers.

"Jenny, you've got to convince her to talk to me. Please, if not for my sake, for our daughter's sake. Little Anna has grown up with the belief that her mother never wanted her or loved her. She's filled with bitterness and resentment toward her like you wouldn't believe. Most of the time, I thought it was deserved, but the scene I witnessed tonight told me it can't be true." Thorn peered deeply into Jenny's eyes, with tears forming in his. "Please, you've got to help me. I can't stand this torment any longer. I must know the truth, so I can be free, and my daughter will be liberated as well. Please say you'll help me."

Jenny saw a man who was desperate to right a wrong. He loved Rose Petal. That had been evident over the past two days, as he had soaked up her presence like a man drinking his last drop of moisture in the desert. He was constantly looking for her, wanting to be around her, and even now trying to gain her approval. Jenny nodded her head yes, letting this desperate man know she would help him.

Thorn squeezed her hand and said, "You've given me hope. I won't forget this. But please, don't let Rose Petal know we've talked, or she may not trust you. Just call me and let me know how things are progressing. Try to find out exactly what she remembers on the day she gave birth to Roseanna. I'm sure there was some sort of mix-up or perhaps even sabotage, looking back and knowing my parents. Do what you can, and call me tomorrow before I fly out. My flight is at 7:00 p.m." Thorn loosened his grip on Jenny's hand.

"Anything I can do, I will, without letting Rose know." Jenny patted Thorn's hand. When she pulled out her phone to call for a ride, Thorn offered her his services. She finished her coffee and stood to leave, as Thorn paid the check. He escorted her to the burgundy-colored pickup truck he'd rented for the weekend. When Jenny started to offer him the address, he reminded her he'd taken her to Rose's already, and the address was in the navigation system.

Once they arrived, he smiled as he opened the door for her. "I really appreciate this, Jenny; I'll make it up to you someday. I want to know everything I can, so I can decide what to do next."

Jenny said good night and walked up the sidewalk to the door. She rang the bell and waited for Rose to answer. A few seconds later, the foyer light came on, and she heard Rose on the other side.

"It's Jenny, Rose. Open the door."

"Are you alone?" Rose's voice quivered.

"Of course, I'm alone. Now let me in. I'm getting cold." She heard the deadbolt move, and the door squeaked open, barely letting her through.

"I-I thought maybe Thorn was out there, trying to get in. He's been calling me all night, so I muted the phone. I never thought about you coming home. I'm sorry. I just noticed you called only a few minutes ago." Rose's face revealed she'd been crying, with her swollen eyelids and reddened nose.

Jenny put her arm around her friend and spoke soothingly, "That's okay. After everything you've been through tonight, I surprised you can even think at all."

It was then Jenny noticed the living room's disheveled appearance. When they left earlier, the house had been spotless, the way Rose always kept it. Now, it appeared like a small tornado had happened. Boxes were strewn around the living room.

Rose followed her friend's eyes and began to explain. "I was looking for it. I knew I had a copy of it somewhere," she started, as she moved to a box and closed the lid.

"Looking for what?" Jenny didn't understand.

"Why Gill, Jr.'s birth certificate, of course. I found it. Naturally, it was in the last box from the garage. Come sit down and look at it. It plainly supports what I said tonight."

Rose was beginning to sound more like herself, but now Jenny was confused. How could Gill, Jr.'s birth certificate solve anything between Rose and Thorn?

It didn't make sense.

# — 21 —

ROSE SHOWED JENNY the birth certificate. As Jenny scanned the document, she came to the section regarding other births. In a square plainly marked by the hospital was the proof that there had been no recorded live births before Gill, Jr. There was one stillborn birth clearly stated on the birth record.

"See? I told him I never gave birth to a live baby other than Gill, Jr. I don't care how he tries to accuse me. Thorn's a liar now just like he was then." Rose seemed to be trying to convince herself as much as she was Jenny.

Jenny sat for a moment staring at the document. Then she calmly asked, "Who supplied the hospital your previous birth history? How did they know about your other birth to begin with?"

That was all it took for Rose to crumple. She sat down like a balloon that had just had all the air let out. She spoke in an almost inaudible voice.

"I told them. They asked a lot of questions before they delivered little Gill. I had a hard delivery with him as well, but nothing compared to the first one. With Thorn's baby, I thought I was going to die. Gill, Jr. had to be taken by caesarean." Rose paused for a moment, growing more and more distressed.

"So, how does this birth certificate solve everything?" Jenny continued to study it, as if Rose's answer might make a difference.

"Oooh! Finding this didn't solve anything, did it? It's still Thorn's word against mine. But I would never lie to my doctor or to anyone else about something as important as this. My baby didn't live." By now, Rose was starting to shake, and tears were streaming down her face. "I would have never given up my baby. They said it was dead, stillborn."

Jenny interjected, "Did the doctor say that? Do you have a record of that baby's death certificate?"

Rose sniffled for a minute and thought. "I don't remember the doctor coming in after that, but I was still groggy from the anesthetic. All I remember is Thorn's parents came in and said the baby had died, and Thorn held me responsible for it. Even though it was stillborn, he never wanted to see or speak to me again. They said he was sorry he'd ever married me. It had been a mistake, and he never wanted to lay eyes on me again. Then they walked out of the hospital room and left me alone.

"I was still dazed from the medicine, and then I was reeling from the news they blurted out to me. They couldn't even wait until I could process the loss of our baby before they let me know Thorn's true feelings. It was by far the worst day of my life. I didn't hurt that bad after the loss of my parents or Gill. I prayed to die right then and there.

"Then, of all the nerve, several minutes later, Thorn came into the room to kiss me good-bye. After everything he had said, I lost it. My temper was out of control from the pain he'd caused me. I never wanted to forgive him. He left the room after a few choice words from me.

"It was about forty-five minutes later when my parents showed up. By then, the Wilder family had left. My folks stayed with me the remainder of the evening."

"The doctor? Surely he came in and spoke with your parents." Jenny couldn't see how the doctor would ignore someone who'd just lost their baby.

"We never saw the doctor again. My parents asked repeatedly to see him. A nurse came and checked on me over the next four days. Finally, on the fourth day after my delivery, the nurse said I was well enough to go home, if someone was there to look after me.

"My parents were glad to get me away from the hospital and back in their care. My mother was very nurturing, and I recovered rather quickly. She did her best to keep me calm and relaxed. After about two-and-a-half weeks at home, I was able to pretty much do what I had done before my pregnancy.

"It was the heartbreak of losing my baby, 'my little wild thorn,' as well as my husband that took forever to heal. I was depressed for months. But it really didn't matter, because my daddy got new orders. Three-and-a-half weeks later, my parents and I were on a plane headed to Germany where we stayed the next three years. I didn't come back to the States until I was twenty-one. By then I had my degree, and I had hardened my heart so it would be almost impossible for me to be hurt again." Rose finished with a deep sigh. "But I never forgot my little Wild Thorn. We'd called the baby that from the time we were married until I went into the delivery room."

# — 22 —

THORN AWAKENED IN his bed in a cold sweat. His dream had been so real. He and Rose Petal were together, and they looked the same as they had at the reunion. They were taking turns holding a little baby girl. But just as he was about to hand the tiny infant to Rose, she smiled at him and walked away. He called out for her to stay, but she kept walking.

That was when he woke up.

Even though he hadn't smoked in over ten years, he wished he had a cigarette. Just one puff would help him relax and forget about life for the moment. That's all he wanted to do right now, forget about life.

This was one of the worst weekends he'd ever faced. He had thought this would be the opportunity that would finally set him free. Instead, he felt more bound up and imprisoned than before. At least before tonight, he had entertained fantasies about how he would confront Rose, and how she would beg for his forgiveness as he walked away the victor. Now, he didn't feel victorious. He felt traumatized. He didn't trust his feelings anymore, because they were telling him one thing, and it conflicted with what he'd been told for years.

He'd believed how bad his Rose Petal was and been devastated by what she'd said to him in that hospital room. But if her version was different than what he'd been told, he needed to know.

Right now, he couldn't discern the truth. Things had gotten too mixed up to know what had really happened. His daughter was full of bitterness from a past that might never have existed. He was still hurting from Rose's cruel words all those years ago, words that taunted him even now in his dreams.

Thorn glanced over at the clock on the hotel nightstand. It was only a few minutes after four. He knew he couldn't sleep anymore, so he got up and headed to the shower. He felt revived as ice cold water washed down his body. Afterwards, he dressed and decided a cup of coffee might finish waking him up.

The Big Griddle closed at 1:00 a.m. and reopened at 4:00 a.m. to allow time for the building to be cleaned and fresh bread and pancake dough to be made for the next day. Thorn left a voicemail with room service to tell his daughter where he was, in the event she woke up and was worried. He got into his truck and headed toward the restaurant.

At least that's where he'd planned to go. But first he made a detour by Rose's. He drove slowly and stared at the darkened house. Only a light at the corner of the garage was on. Thorn let out a deep sigh and headed to the restaurant.

As he pulled in the parking lot, he noticed only a handful of cars were there. Parking his rented truck in the semi-darkness, he headed to the door. Stepping inside, the hostess immediately seated him. As he passed the first booth, he heard a squeak and immediately turned his attention in the direction of the sound.

There sat Jenny and Rose Petal.

The air went out of Thorn's lungs. He just stared at the couple sitting in the booth. Rose's hair was damp, as if she'd showered recently. Jenny's eyes looked like she was doing all she could to keep them forced open.

The waitress noticed the group had an obvious connection, and she asked. "Would you care to sit here, sir?" She pointed to the open space by Rose.

Thorn couldn't believe his luck, and he mutely nodded his head.

ROSE HAD SEEN Thorn walk in, and she saw the waitress question him, looking their way. She muttered to herself, "He wouldn't dare try to do this!"

Jenny stared at the floor, not wanting to get caught in the crossfire between these two.

Thorn's face had a tormented look. His eyes dared Rose to deny him access to her booth.

Rose was curt, her words aimed at the waitress, Jenny, and Thorn. "It's a free country. I guess he can sit wherever he chooses."

She couldn't believe he had the gall to speak to her after everything that had just happened only a few hours ago. She thought she'd made it clear that she never wanted to be near him again.

Right now, she didn't want to face Thornton Jebulon Wilder or listen to anything he might have to say.

THORN WASN'T ABOUT to be intimidated, especially after the dream he'd had of them. There was no way Rose was getting the upper hand in this situation. He could goad her right back, and he did.

"Well, Rose Darlin'." Thorn took a deep breath. "Since you put it that way, I believe I will sit here."

At that, he dropped into the seat, almost dislodging Rose, as the cushion shifted under his weight. He glanced at her and smiled, his eyebrows lifting in mirth. Jenny covered her mouth and tried her best not to laugh, as did the waitress.

ROSE GREW HOT and clenched her teeth. She was furious, but she wouldn't let Thorn break her. He'd done so once, but she was stronger than he was now.

AS THE WAITRESS left to get Thorn's cup of cof-

fee, tension swirled inside the booth. Why of all plac-
es, and at this premature hour, did Thorn have to
show up here? What reason did Rose Petal have to be
up so early? These questions plagued both Rose and
Thorn as they sat beside each other in the crowded
booth. However, their shoulders were touching, and
part of the tension came from the fire shooting from
that electric physical contact.

JENNY WATCHED THE scene. As tired as she was,
she could tell. A storm was brewing, and the lightning
was about to fly.

# — 23 —

ANNA AWAKENED MUCH earlier than usual.

She blamed it on the chain of events from the previous evening. Seeing her mother for the first time was a shock. Then her blatant denial of Anna's existence had infuriated Anna even more. Finally, to watch her dad almost take that woman's side was even more exasperating.

She would be relieved when this town was nothing more than a bad memory, and she could put all this behind her. She just wanted to get on with her life. At the thought of life, Anna rubbed her still-flat belly. Deep within, she could feel the new life beginning inside her.

That had been part of the reason she'd been anxious these past two weeks to meet her birth mother.

Now that she was finally pregnant with her own child, she wanted to see who her baby might resemble. Anna had never seen a picture of her birth mother, so she didn't know just which traits had come to her from her father and which from her mother.

After seeing the woman her father claimed was her mother, she had no doubts. Anna knew she was the spitting image of her except for her height and hair. Her mother was beautiful even now, and it was understandable why her father had fallen in love with her so long ago. She could only imagine how gorgeous she'd been in her youth. It was no wonder he had married so young. It was also obvious that beauty didn't always go with outstanding character.

Anna was only six weeks pregnant, but she already felt a bond to the small being sharing her body. She'd be thirty-nine in January, and her baby was due in June. She felt the excitement of becoming a mother. At the same time, she felt a deep resentment toward her own biological mother. How could she have not wanted Anna, her own child, her flesh and blood, after all the months of carrying her in her body? Anna couldn't comprehend the thought of not wanting her baby after only six weeks. Her grandmother had said her mother didn't even want to look at her and didn't ask if she was a boy or a girl. At the same time, her grandmother repeatedly reminded her of how much she was loved by her grandparents and her father.

She knew her dad had come to this reunion for closure. He had never been what she would call happy, not in his personal life. He'd tried, having been married a couple of times she knew of, besides his first. Not living with him, it had been hard for her to keep track. The marriages always ended in divorce. But he never seemed overly sad or disappointed about it. He appeared numb to any emotion toward anyone except his daughter.

Then, last night, for the first time, Anna saw her father reacting differently to a woman. Something had caused his emotions to kindle. Even Anna could see that. When Rose's knees had buckled under her, he had been worried, and it had showed. Without even thinking, he had grabbed her and carried her to the sofa. He barked orders for someone to get water for him. He'd sat there and given her sips from the cup, nursing her until she opened her eyes.

It was when Anna saw the sigh of relief on her father's face that she knew the emotional attachment he still felt to his first love. It was like no other expression she'd ever seen. He was totally euphoric as Rose's eyes fluttered open. It was obvious he still had deeply rooted feelings her.

That was what worried Anna now. Would he be able to walk away from her once and for all with her denial about Anna? It would be trying over the next few hours to see how her father fared after all the excitement died down. Her father alone with his feelings of betrayal and abandonment wasn't a good thing. That was what this weekend was supposed to help heal, but from what she saw last night, all it did was ignite a bonfire from smoldering ashes. And now it was her job to try to put that fire back out and kill it for good. She couldn't let her father continue to long for something that would never be. If his old love had hurt him before, she'd do it again. Anna had to prevent that.

She hoped she was up to the task.

She also knew she'd have to tell her father soon about her own pregnancy, despite her separation from Sam a little over a month ago. That was something else she wasn't looking forward to. Now, she needed to see if she could catch her dad at The Big Griddle for breakfast. His message indicated he'd been there about forty-five minutes. If she was lucky, she could catch him before he left for the hotel.

# — 24 —

THORN JUST STARED at Rosemary, and he refused to budge an inch. Rose could feel his eyes boring a hole through her, but she still refused to look his direction. She was praying for strength and for God to give her wisdom. Every time she'd opened her mouth all weekend, she'd let her old emotions and lack of self-control lash out. She always felt guilty later. After her sarcastic comment earlier, she thought it would be best if she kept her mouth shut, no matter how Thorn baited her. Then and only then would he know she'd changed.

She wanted him to see she wasn't the same emotional teenager she'd been when he walked out on her all those years ago. God had truly helped her become a better mother, grandmother, and overall person. Of course, when it came to Thorn, she seemed to immediately become reactionary, and all thoughts of self-control seemed to fly out the window.

What was it the Apostle Paul said? What I don't want to do, I find myself doing, and what I want to do, I don't. Did he know humanity or what? That was exactly how Rosemary felt while Thorn's bulky frame filled the booth.

The waitress arrived with two black coffees and one water. Jenny groaned, accepting a cup of coffee. She muttered that it didn't matter if she couldn't get back to sleep. Everyone could survive on three hours a night, right?

JENNY DECIDED ROSE had good instincts, because they weren't there five minutes, and Thorn showed up. She could tell he'd freshly showered by his damp hair. It was obvious they were both wide awake by the way they tapped the table, all the while ignoring one another.

The waitress delivered their drinks and asked them if they were ready to order. Jenny requested a bagel with cream cheese. With the coffee, she would never get back to sleep if she ate any more than that.

THORN ORDERED BISCUITS and gravy. Rose ordered a single toast. Thorn looked at the waitress and back to Rose. He wasn't satisfied with Rose's meager selection, but she could order whatever she wanted. He couldn't control that.

"What else do you want?" he demanded gruffly, not meaning food. Rose shot him a sideways glance. She had ignored him as much as she could. However, this was a direct question, and Thorn intended to force her hand.

"I already told the waitress what I want."

Rose referred to the toast. Thorn was thinking of the vicious words she'd said at the reunion. They still preyed on his mind and heart.

"Do you really mean it, Rose Petal?" he questioned, in a much more subdued tone.

"Are you deaf? All I want is toast. I'm still too nervous from everything that's happened to eat anything else."

ROSE FINALLY LOOKED at him. She saw a myriad of emotions on his face. She could tell he was in torment, but what did that have to do with toast?

What did he think she meant?

THORN SAW HER trying to read his facial expressions, and in his relief at realizing he'd misunderstood her answer, he broke into a huge smile. Rose blushed, turned her head away, and looked at the other side of the booth at Jenny.

Maybe she hadn't been trying to hurt him intentionally just then.

The waitress finally broke in, "So, is there anything else?"

"No," Thorn said almost cheerily. "We're good

here." He continued to tap on the table, but it was a much lighter sound, matching the lighter mood in his heart.

JENNY NEEDED TO get Thorn's attention without Rose noticing. However, like always, he was caught up with Rose and only Rose.

Jenny wondered how this couple had ever managed to break up with the way they acted around each other. It was as if someone had sabotaged their relationship. They had been so much in love back then. There was no way either of them would have given up the other without a fight.

Even now they were like lovestruck teenagers. They were always aware of each other's presence, even if it wasn't acknowledged.

THORN PUT HIS arm across the back of the booth. He wasn't exactly touching Rose, but he wasn't exactly not touching her, either. Rose could feel his arm on the back of the booth, but she tried to ignore it. If she moved, he'd know it bothered her, and then he'd know he was having an effect on her.

She tried not to respond as his arm slowly slipped down until it was touching her shoulders. Then she felt his hand ever so softly stroking her hair. That was the last straw. She knew she'd overreacted at the reunion. Honestly, the joke was the worst thing anyone could ever pull, but Thorn had always been crass like that. Still, he'd insulted her, called her a liar, and now he thought it was okay to touch her hair.

This wouldn't do.

"Excuse me, Thorn. I believe I need to go wash my hands." Rose spoke to him in an even-keeled tone. She would keep her voice under control, even if he was infuriating her.

THORN GLANCED AT Rose, gave a crooked grin, and climbed out of the booth. He turned and helped her out, holding her hand a little too long. She simply stared at him until he released it. Rose then headed to the ladies' restroom. The timing could not have been better, creating a perfect opportunity for Jenny. She quickly drew open her purse and spoke in a hushed tone.

"Thorn, quick. Get a load of this. It's Gill, Jr's birth certificate. I think you're in for a big surprise. It may answer some questions about the past and start you thinking about new ones."

# — 25 —

A DARK LOOK swept across Thorn's face as he read the document.

"Where did you get this?" he demanded.

"Rose had it when I got to her house. She'd been looking for it ever since she returned from the banquet. She immediately showed it to me to prove her story was true. The only problem is, she admitted she was the one who supplied the hospital with the information about your daughter's birth. However, she truly believes this is the truth. She insists that you left her."

Jenny had barely finished speaking when she saw Rose returning from the restroom. Jenny reached for the paper, but Thorn pleaded, "Let me keep this for a few days. I promise I'll return it in mint condition.

Please." He slipped it into his jeans pocket as Rose approached their table.

"WHAT, DID I hear Thorn Wilder say please? Surely my ears are playing tricks on me. I didn't even know that word was in his vocabulary." Rose dripped acid with her words.

"You'd be surprised by a lot I'd say, if you were around me more," Thorn replied in a soft, deep voice, as he stepped from the table to let her be seated.

Rose looked at him. She didn't want to be cornered by him in that booth again. She turned to Jenny, who was preoccupied with not watching either of them. Rose sighed. At least she wasn't alone with him.

Thorn waited, giving Rose that look again, the one that made her think she was about to be his breakfast, he was so hungry for her. All she could do was scoot in next to him in silence. She was afraid to utter anything regarding his last remark.

Thorn carefully sat back down. This time Rose didn't come bouncing off the seat. Jenny glanced up and cracked a smile, saying nothing.

THEIR FOOD ARRIVED, and no one said anything while they ate. Jenny was so sleepy she could barely spread her cream cheese on her bagel. Thorn and Rose seemed not to notice. Thorn was busy looking sideways at Rose nibbling on her toast, looking totally content. He consumed his biscuits and gravy in only a few bites, and he flagged the waitress down to order more coffee.

Rose on the other hand was taking very measured breaths. She wasn't letting Thorn bother her in any way. She would maintain control of her emotions around him regardless of how he behaved.

Jenny finally finished her breakfast and was ready to go. She was too tired to really pay attention to the sparring couple. She needed to get back to Rose's and get some much-needed rest before she went to see her brother that afternoon, and she no longer thought Rose would want to accompany her.

She spoke up, "I don't know about you two, but I'm sleepy and would like to take a nap before I go to see my brother this afternoon. So, Rose, if you don't mind, do you think you could take me home?"

ROSE BREATHED A sigh of relief. This was just the out she'd been waiting for. "Sure, I'm ready right now. Let's go." Rose shot a glance at Thorn as she asked, "If you'll excuse me, I need to get Jenny home, and then I want to get ready for church."

Thorn cut his dark eyes at Rose, responding, "Sure, Rose Petal. Anything you want." He slowly stood and helped Rose from the booth, his massive frame towering over her. Thorn got out his wallet to pay the check. Rose stopped him and said, "We were here first, so we'll pay this time."

"Then I'll get the tip," he replied, as he pulled out a twenty.

Jenny turned, smiled at him, and said it was good to see him. She said she hoped it wasn't another forty years before they got together again. Thorn repeated almost the same thing to her and laughed as he gave her a hug good-bye.

Rose tried to slip by Thorn undetected, but her purse got caught between his knee and Jenny as Thorn hugged her good-bye. Rose had no choice but to wait until they had finished their salutations.

Then Thorn turned to her. But instead of saying or doing anything, he took her hand and pulled her toward the door, leaving Jenny at the counter paying the check. Once outside in the shadows of the early morning, Thorn again lifted Rose off her feet and held her in his arms.

"Oh, Rose Petal. You're like a bad habit for me. I can't seem to break it no matter how hard I try." Then Thorn kissed her very gently on the forehead and set her down. "But I'm trying. Honestly, I am."

Rose was speechless as she regained her poise. Thorn looked at her, waiting silently, as Jenny came out to Rose's car, and they got in and left. Once they disappeared, Thorn walked toward his truck.

TWO ROWS DOWN, a very shocked Anna had witnessed the entire scene from her rental car. She knew, now. Her daddy was in deep, maybe too deep for anyone's help this time. Grandpa and Grandma weren't here to save him this go round. But from the looks of things, it didn't appear he wanted anyone's help at all.

# — 26 —

"THANKS, JENNY. YOU were a real lifesaver getting us out of The Big Griddle so quickly." Rose patted her friend on the arm, profuse in her gratitude.

Jenny mumbled, "You're welcome," as she tried to stay awake on the way back to her friend's home. There was no traffic at that early hour, and they arrived at Rose's house in less than twenty minutes.

By the time Rose opened the door and turned off the alarm, Jenny was already headed to the guest bedroom. She quickly changed into her sleeping shorts and was off to bed. Being in the middle of Rose and Thorn's tumultuous relationship had taken a toll on her. She couldn't keep pace with their emotional roller coaster connection. As soon as her head hit the pillow, she was asleep.

Rose, on the other hand, was completely awake, with adrenalin coursing through her veins. Thorn had surprised her by not being his usual aggressive self. He'd seemed to consider her feelings. It was as if he had changed from an ogre to a human in just a few short hours.

She snuggled into her favorite chair in the family room and thanked God for the change He'd brought about, not only in her, but also in Thorn. She knew it took someone greater than them to help keep their emotions in check. She picked up her Bible from the coffee table where she left it each day after reading her devotionals and opened it to the verse that said, "All things work together for good to them who love the Lord and are called according to his purpose." She thought about what God was saying to her in that verse. It meant that in every situation, God would use the events for good in her life. That meant even this weekend with Thorn. According to God's Word, it would, in some way, bring something positive into her life. Rose closed her eyes and smiled. God would truly have to do a miracle for that to happen.

HER RINGING PHONE woke her. Roxanne was on the line.

"Are you going to church this morning? If so, do you want us to pick you up?"

"Well, um . . ." Rose tried to focus on the time but couldn't think where she'd put her watch.

Roxanne asked Jack a question Rose couldn't

hear, and then she continued, "I still haven't got my make-up on or my hair done. It would be at least half an hour before we could come by. Would you like that?"

"That will be perfect. I'll leave the car for Jenny, if she wakes up and decides to go early to see her brother. I'll see you in about thirty minutes." Rose hung up the phone and found her watch on the chair-side table. She was relieved to see she'd been asleep for almost three hours.

She hurried to her bedroom, trying to decide what to wear. She considered one of her more casual out-fits, because she was short on time and wouldn't need to put on hose. She had a couple of almost floor length cotton print dresses. She selected one with tur-quoise accents, to go with her new sandals and match-ing purse.

She quickly applied her make-up, using what Jen-ny had left in her bathroom last night. She was spray-ing cologne when she heard her cell phone ring. She answered to Roxanne on the line.

"Honey, we're right outside. Are you still plan-ning on riding with us? If you're short on time, we can go on, if you want."

Rose asked them to wait just a minute, and she scribbled a note to Jenny and attached it to her door. Rose closed the front door after her, making sure it was locked, and she hurried outside to Jack and Roxanne's waiting car.

They arrived at church with only minutes to spare

before the morning service. They usually made it to Sunday school as well, but after the debacle yesterday, they couldn't feel too guilty. The threesome found their way inside and were pleased to see their usual spot unoccupied as they slid into their seats.

Different ones waved and smiled across the congregation as they sat down. They noticed some were continuing to smile and wave, and when they turned to see, they discovered Thorn coming down their aisle. It seemed he was heading right for their pew.

As he stepped next to Rose, he asked, "Mind if I join you?"

Rose was too bewildered to answer the question.

Roxanne's jaw dropped, and Jack scratched his head, as he leaned around and answered, "Of course not. We're glad you could be here."

Thoughts swirled in Rose's head. What was Thorn doing at her church? Didn't he know this was a house of God?

The senior pastor opened with prayer. Rose was so taken back by Thorn's appearance she hardly heard the poignant words resonating through the hushed sanctuary until the loud "Amen" was repeated by the worshippers. Thorn's deep voice vibrated in her ears as he affirmed the prayer with the rest of the congregation. Rose was more surprised than ever, first that Thorn would even be in church, but more so that he would give a confirming word at the end of the prayer.

The praise and worship service began with several

new choruses interspersed with traditional hymns. Surprisingly, Thorn kept up with most of the music. Rose did her best to concentrate on the service, but it was next to impossible with Thorn at her side. She could feel him glancing at her from time to time, and his breath brushed her forehead as he sang some of the songs.

She was acutely uncomfortable.

Roxanne reached over and squeezed her hand for support. That helped some. But for the most part, she felt like it was just Thorn and her standing alone in the vast building.

Finally, the congregation was seated, and the offertory prayer was given. A beautiful hymn was played. Thorn bumped Rose getting out his billfold, and she did her best to ignore the simple brush of his leg against hers.

Even here in church, she felt a current of electricity rush through her.

# — 27 —

AS THE SERVICE continued, Thorn became more relaxed. His parents were Christians, but he had been raised in a more formal faith. They had attended every Sunday morning. His mother had served on the local church board. No matter where they were stationed in the U.S., his parents had always located a church they felt comfortable with and transferred their membership to that congregation.

In contrast, Rose's church with its more relaxed atmosphere and feeling of family made Thorn wish this was how he'd been brought up. The pastor gave a simple message of faith, hope, and peace. He didn't use a lot of flowery words or disconnected stories. His straightforward approach touched Thorn's heart. He then gave an invitation to anyone who would like to have the peace he spoke about to join him at the front.

Thorn thought about all the years of unhappiness he'd experienced. He remembered all the hurts and disappointments he'd survived. He was tired of carrying the burdens himself. If what this pastor said was true, he could rid himself of all his cumbersome emotional weights once and for all. He wouldn't have to use Rose to have closure in his life. God would take care of that for him.

Without another thought, he stood and made his way to the front of the church where a few others had already gathered. The pastor and several members collected around each individual and prayed with them. The senior pastor came and stood with Thorn. He questioned him about his salvation. The minister offered him a new relationship with God and the world around him.

Thorn accepted Christ as his personal savior and released his past to him. He felt like he was a newborn baby. All the cares of the world seemed to float away. Never in his life had he felt like he was finally free of all the entanglements life had bound him up with. Tears of joy streamed down his face. He was exactly what the pastor had described, a new creature in Christ.

Everyone at the front of the church hugged him, while the congregation cheered for the new converts. It felt to Thorn as though he was the only one there. Then he looked where he'd been sitting. Jack and

Roxanne were still there, but Rose was gone.

ROSE HAD QUIETLY disappeared as soon as Thorn went forward. She was in the ladies' lounge trying to process the series of events taking place in the auditorium.

Did Thorn really intend to accept Christ as his savior, or was he doing this as a show to impress her? What made Thorn pick this day and this time to make a decision for Christ? She had so many doubts about herself, how could she trust anyone else?

When she emerged from the lounge, the first person she saw was Roxanne. Her friend stepped up to her and put her arm around her shoulder.

"There you are. We were beginning to think you had walked home. Are you okay? We were getting worried about you, especially Thorn. Isn't this wonderful, that he got saved today? After everything that happened at the reunion, Thorn's changed his life around." Roxanne seemed to bubble with joy and enthusiasm.

Rose fought her emotions as she pulled her friend back into the lounge. She wanted to speak her mind, but not in front of the entire church. Once inside, she let her anger erupt.

"Oh, yeah. That's great for him. He can just walk away guilt-free and not be responsible for anything in his past." Rose spat the words with an edge. She hardly believed Thorn would change, and she was sure her face told her feelings.

Her attitude took Roxanne by surprise. "Why, Rose. I thought you'd be pleased with anyone who found Christ as his savior. I'm really disappointed by your reaction."

Rose felt her eyes burn with emotion. She knew she should be overjoyed about anyone who entered the kingdom, but this was Thorn. He couldn't be trusted.

She turned to Roxanne, "I am. It's just that, well, I'm not sure I believe Thorn's confession is real. He's done so many things to hurt me, I wouldn't put anything past him." She paused to run her fingers around her eyes, and then she continued, "I truly hope his decision for Christ is genuine."

"All we can do his pray for him. He'll need it, judging by his daughter's behavior last night," Roxanne added, as they exited the ladies' lounge. Rose said nothing, but in her mind, there was no daughter, just a cruel hoax.

They headed to the parking lot and found Jack waiting for them. Thorn was nowhere to be seen. Rose breathed a sigh of relief. At least she wouldn't have to face him right now. If she was lucky, she might be able to avoid him altogether. She hadn't seen him for forty years, so why not make it another forty before they made contact again?

# — 28 —

THORN PULLED INTO the hotel parking lot. The sign towered over the building, and it caught the sun, reflecting it onto the cars in the lot. Several high clouds danced across the sky, caught in wind currents that had yet to make it to ground level. He drove past several vehicles until he came to an empty spot just down from the entrance. He had a lot on his mind he wanted to share with his daughter. He used the key fob to lock the truck and headed inside through the glass entrance doors. Waiting on the elevator, he whistled a light-hearted tune, and he greeted the couple exiting before stepping inside and pressing the button for his floor. He whistled a new tune as he approached Anna's door. After a quick knock, he identified himself, and his daughter let him in.

"How's Sam doing these days?" Thorn smiled as he inquired politely. "I know he's been working out of town, and I'm sorry he couldn't come with you."

"I suppose he's fine. I haven't spoken with him today. Don't you look all bright and shining? Daddy, where have you been? I hope it's not out with her. She broke your heart before, and she'll do it again. I know her kind, and so did Grandmother."

Thorn listened patiently, and he continued to smile and wait for his daughter to finish her tirade. He knew she didn't like her mother, but that was based on the information she'd been fed by her grandmother. He was here to set the record straight, as well as to tell her about his newfound faith. One had everything to do with Rose, and the other had nothing to do with his Rose Petal.

Finally, Anna stopped and stared at him. "You haven't heard a word I just said, have you?"

"Well, most of it," her father admitted, with a sheepish grin. "But what I want to know is if you're going to listen to me." Thorn searched his daughter's face for an answer.

"I always listen to you; I just don't always follow your advice," Anna replied honestly, looking intently into her father's eyes.

"This is one time I really want you to pay close attention to what I'm about to say." Thorn knew it was vital to have her focused on his words and not on her feelings about Rose.

ANNA COULD TELL by the somber expression he wore that her dad had something of importance he wanted to share. She sat on the bed across from him, pulling one leg under her. "Okay, Dad. I'm ready."

Thorn leaned forward, resting his elbows on his knees. "This morning, for the first time in a long time, I went to church. It wasn't for the right reason. I went to see Rose Petal.

"I knew she attended that particular church, because Jack had told me the three of them went together. Jack and Roxanne have been members there for years. Rose just started attending this past year. While I was there, something wonderful happened." Thorn reached across and took his daughter's hand as he spoke.

"Anna, I accepted Christ as my personal savior and have been born again." He stopped and wiped a lone tear from one eye. "It's the greatest feeling I've ever experienced in my life. Just knowing I don't have to fight my battles alone, and that my past is forgiven forever is almost unbelievable." Thorn took time to pull a tissue from the bedside table and pat his eyes. "This has nothing to do with your mother and me; this has to do with a new relationship between God and me. I'm a true Christian now, honey."

Anna couldn't believe what she was hearing. Her father had gotten religion and was now calling himself a Christian? He'd abandoned that years ago.

"Did she coerce you to do this? What feminine wiles did she pull to get you into this position?" Anna didn't believe this at all, and she pressed her father for answers. "I've seen her in action, and she's pretty slick. She had to have said or done something that would make you want to become a Christian."

Anna's laced her tirade with sarcasm, and she stood and faced the window. The shears were drawn, but the light-blocking shades were open, and she could see hazy activity on the streets.

"Actually, sweetie, she had nothing to do with it. She won't talk to me, and she certainly didn't want me to sit by her during the service. It was just knowing how tired I am of everything in my life. I've wanted a change for a long time. I just didn't know how to go about it. When the pastor spoke this morning with such conviction and assurance, I knew what I wanted. So, I went to the front and gave my heart and life to God. When I went back to my seat, Rose Petal wasn't there, and I haven't seen her since." Thorn peered into his daughter's face, as if trying to read her thoughts.

Anna just stared back, astonished by what she'd heard. Her father's ex-wife had nothing to do with his decision; he'd done it all on his own. Wasn't that a hoot? Maybe it was just leftover desire from the parking lot this morning. Anna knew her dad must be trying to impress his first wife, even if he wasn't aware of it. She hoped he wasn't desperate enough to do something even more rash just to make an impact on her.

"Dad, let me clarify, you're sure you're not doing

this to get, hmm, my *mother's* attention?" She had a difficult time saying the word.

"Anna, it's like I told you. My decision for Christ has nothing to do with my relationship with your mother, who by the way really thought you were still-born."

The change of subject immediately stirred Anna's emotions. "Just because she says something doesn't make it true. I don't care how hard you try to convince me, Dad. It just won't work." She lashed out at him. "You've never denied what Grandma and Grandpa said. Why now are you suddenly having second thoughts?" She flipped her hair as she glared at him.

"One reason is the expression she wore when she saw you and tried to put the pieces of the puzzle together. The other reason is this." Thorn reached into his pocket and pulled out the birth certificate that Jenny had given him. He carefully unfolded it. "Read this," he said, as he pushed it into his daughter's hand.

Anna glanced at it. "Who is Gilland James Bruton, Jr, and why do you have his birth certificate?"

"He's Rose Petal's son, your half-brother." Thorn spoke quietly.

Anna was silent as she studied the document for several seconds. "So, what am I supposed to be looking for?"

Thorn reached to point out the part where it showed a previous stillborn birth.

Anna handed it back to him and laughed. "This doesn't prove anything. Anyone can forge these."

Her father replied, "I know. That's why I'm going to the county tomorrow and get another one issued. This one is notarized, so I believe it's real. But I intend to make sure."

"You can do anything you want, Dad, but it still won't convince me. Maybe she didn't want a girl, and that's why she kept her other baby. After all, it was a boy. All I know is she didn't want me, period."

"OH, HONEY, YOU can't know that." Thorn wanted to give his daughter a hug, but before he could stand, she turned to him with pain on her face.

"You can betray my love for you and try to get back with her, but I'll never be a part of her life. She didn't want me then, and I don't want her now." Anna's voice was ragged, and her eyes were on the edge of tears. She finished in a torrent of emotion, finally releasing tears to gush down her cheeks.

Thorn leaped to his feet and hugged his daughter close. He loved her more than anything. He didn't want to do anything to hurt her, but he had to find answers of his own. He had to know the truth, and the more he thought about it, the more he realized how naïve he'd been. He'd never tried to talk to Rose after that one time, taking everything his parents had said as truth.

Now, looking back, he'd never do that as an adult. He would have questioned her himself and made her say she didn't love him or want him ever again. Holding his daughter and feeling her pain made him more determined than ever to get to the bottom of this unresolved issue that had eaten forty years of their lives.

He would start tomorrow. He wasn't leaving town until the truth was known, no matter how ugly or sordid it was.

# — 29 —

"BY THE WAY, I saw you this morning at The Big Griddle." Anna said the words as an accusation, and also to make her father aware she wasn't clueless.

Thorn smiled as he patted Anna's arm. "I saw you, too, sitting in your car. If you hadn't been there staring, a whole lot more might have happened between your mother and me."

"But Daddy, you had her in your arms. She wasn't even touching the ground."

"I know. That way, Rose Petal couldn't get away. I've always had to do that to keep her captive. She's never been the type to come after me."

"Daddy!"

"It's not something I was even aware of before I came to the reunion, but the truth is, Anna, I still love

Rose Petal. I think I have all these years. I think that's the reason I've never been happy with anyone else, no matter how hard they tried to love me. I just didn't love them the way I love your mother. She does something to me no other woman can."

"How can you love someone who's mean and hurtful and just uses people to get her way?" Anna's bitterness pierced her words.

Thorn thought for a moment before answering. "I think it must be the way God loves us. Unconditionally. He sees our true heart, the one He created for loving Him. That's why I was so relieved to become a part of His love today. According to the pastor, He never gives up on us. God is always there waiting to accept us as we are. Sure, your mother and I had problems in our marriage. We were so young and inexperienced, but I always loved her, and I believe she loved me."

"You can't mean that, after what she did." Anna was incredulous.

Thorn paused for a second and gave the only answer he had to give. "I'm the one who loved her. Your grandparents always disliked her immensely."

"It's because they saw her for what she was, a user," Anna spat.

"How was she a user, Anna? Was it her idea to get pregnant? No, she's the one who begged me to wait and tried to get me to slow down. She never attempted anything to persuade me to be intimate with her. Her parents were very strict. She had to dress very modestly and be in by ten on a date night.

"We only stayed out late because of the prom, and it was only that one time. Then it was her parents that came and confronted mine about doing the right thing. Your grandparents didn't want us to marry. They just wanted her family stationed elsewhere, content for her to have the baby by herself, illegitimate or not. But I loved her, Anna. I loved your mother. We got married, despite my parents. And those next seven months were the happiest in my life. No, your mother didn't use me. If anything, I used her."

Anna dropped on the bed. This wasn't what she'd expected. Her father wasn't just in love with her mother, but he was deeply in love with her. He defended her on every turn. He was telling stories that were totally contrary to her grandparents' tales. Surely her Dad didn't expect her to think everything he was saying was true.

"So, how long are you going to stay here?" Anna needed to know how bad this could get.

"Until I get the whole truth and the answers to every question I have about my marriage, your birth, and my divorce from your mother." Thorn spoke with such conviction it startled his daughter. "So, however long that is, that's how long I'll be here. It might be a week or maybe a month, I don't know. But when I do leave, it'll be because my heart and mind are both satisfied."

Anna sighed. He was grown up, after all. She knew she didn't have enough power over him to change this, and she did have a flight to catch.

"I guess your mind is made up. Will you at least take me to the airport, so I can catch my plane back home?" She was no longer sure how her father would answer.

"Of course, sweetie. I'll be happy to see you off. Will Sam be there to pick you up? You know I wouldn't leave you stranded. You may not understand this right now, but I'm doing this for the both of us. When I get back, I'll be a better person. I want us to be able to enjoy the rest of our lives without any regrets. It's because I love you so much that I have to do this."

"Don't you worry about Sam." She laughed sourly. "Thanks, Daddy. I know you love me, and I appreciate it. I love you, too."

THORN SMILED AT Anna as he spoke. He loved his daughter and wanted her to know the truth, so they could both find peace and contentment in their future.

# — 30 —

ROSE WAS UP and dressed when she heard Jenny pull into the driveway. Her friend had left to see her brother before Rose returned from church, and Rose was grateful. She had needed a nap, and her exhaustion had taken over. Not only was she physically tired, but also drained emotionally from her confrontation with Thorn during the service. She had barely gotten in the door and eaten a sandwich, before she found herself dozing off in the living room. She'd given up, undressed, and crawled into her bed.

Now she felt much better. She glanced at the clock, realizing she'd slept nearly four hours. Jenny rang the doorbell, and when Rose unlocked the door, she came through with a smile on her face.

"Thanks for loaning me your car. It was so good

to see my brother again. I hardly recognized my own niece, she looks so much like an adult now. It's amazing how time passes so quickly. And speaking of time, I've got to get my things together and get to the airport pretty soon."

"Yes, we need to leave in the next forty-five minutes to be there to catch your flight. Praise God, there are no showers predicted for your flight home. That's the last thing you need after a weekend like this."

Jenny nodded her head and went straight to the guest room to gather her things. Minutes later she reappeared, ready to depart. "Do you mind if we stop and grab a few snacks for the flight? I don't want my blood sugar to get out of whack."

"Of course, not. I'll be happy to stop on the way," Rose replied with a smile.

Minutes later, they were headed for the terminal and Jenny's flight home. Rose insisted on helping Jenny check her bags with the skycap. As they approached the check-in booth, they both stopped short.

Directly in front of them were Thorn and his daughter. Even from a distance, there was no mistaking her resemblance to Rose. Without all the heavy make-up from the banquet, it was easy to see her defined cheekbones and large eyes. Her slightly turned-up nose was an exact copy of Rose's.

Rose swallowed hard, as Jenny squeezed her hand and said, "Don't worry, they'll be gone in just a few minutes, and your life will get back to normal. Just hang on a little longer, and this whole ordeal will be over."

Rose nodded and drew in another sharp breath. They watched as Thorn hugged his daughter good-bye, and she headed through airport security. Jenny and Rose checked Jenny's bags, and Jenny gave Rose a quick hug and reassured her Thorn would be gone soon, as well. Then she stepped through security and toward her flight.

No sooner had Jenny disappeared out of sight than Rose heard Thorn, or felt him, or perhaps it was a lit-tle of both. He was there beside her walking in step with her toward her car.

"Did you stay to see Jenny off?" he questioned her, in a conversational and pleasant tone.

"Yes," she replied brusquely, hoping he'd tell her he would be checking his bags and heading through security soon. Rose continued toward her car and her life without him. Thorn kept up the easy pace next to her. Finally, exasperated, she turned and questioned him, "What time is your plane departure?"

"Oh, Rose Petal, I'm not going anywhere for a while. There's too many memories here I want to ex-plore. I plan to stay in our little town until I get all the answers I want." With that, he smiled and put his arm around her waist, stopping her in her tracks.

"Thorn, this isn't appropriate." She glanced around to see who might be watching.

"Rose, hear me out. Something happened in your church that's never happened in my life before. I feel different. I tried to explain it to Anna, but she refused to accept it. She thinks it's some plot you're using against me, or that I'm trying to win you with this so-called religion. But it's neither." He gave Rose one of his piercing gazes. "I've accepted Christ as my savior, Rose, and now I need to know that you've forgiven me as well. I think we need to have a long and serious talk about what happened forty years ago."

Rose just stared at him. Why would he want to have a talk now? There was nothing left to say. She just wanted him to go away. She was glad he'd found Jesus, but he needed to share his newfound joy somewhere else.

"Well, what do you say? Is there?" Thorn probed her, as if she hadn't been listening.

"Oh, uh, Thorn. I didn't hear you. What did you ask?" Rose was infuriated that this man could make her lose focus like that.

Thorn repeated, "I asked you if there was a place where we could be in private, undisturbed by anyone or anything. I would offer my hotel room, but I think it might be a little uncomfortable with just a king size bed. I didn't order the suite like our daughter did."

"There's no daughter, Thorn, and I can't believe you expect me to want to discuss anything with you after this weekend." Rose took in a deep breath and turned from him, wincing at the word "our." Why was he playing these mind games with her? What was he trying to accomplish?

"All I want to do is talk, Rose; honestly, I need to

know the truth from your lips, not what someone told me you said. I made that mistake before, and I won't let it happen again."

Rose turned to look at him. His jaw was set, and his face was determined. She'd seen that expression enough in their brief marriage to realize he was through talking about it. Only action would do now. She wouldn't have any peace from him unless she talked with him, even though there was nothing to say. He would keep bugging her, and she really wanted this to be over. She couldn't take much more of Thorn without something happening.

She also wanted to get home, so she agreed to have him meet her at her house in an hour.

# — 31 —

THE FIRST THING on Rose's list once she got home was to freshen up. Afterward, she made a pitcher of iced tea and cut a slice of lemon meringue pie from the one she'd kept at home. With that in front of Thorn, maybe he'd have something to do besides think of ways to lie to her. When the doorbell rang nearly an hour later, she said a prayer, took a deep breath, and opened the door.

Thorn took up the whole opening with his broad shoulders.

"Come into the kitchen. I thought we'd be more comfortable there," Rose offered.

THORN FOLLOWED HER to the breakfast nook and to the waiting piece of pie and iced tea. He sat down slowly and let his whole body relax.

This was what he'd always wanted, to be with Rose, together and alone. It felt like home to him. No man could ever ask for more than the love of a sweet woman. That's what Rose had always been, sweet. Even when she was angry, he thought she was cute, and he'd told her so.

That, of course, only made her angrier, and she'd often start a fight that would end up with them falling asleep in each other's arms. That antique brass bed was only a double. He'd slept at an angle with Rose in his arms, so she wouldn't tumble off.

The memory of them together made him smile.

ROSE ON THE other hand was uncomfortable in the silence of her kitchen. She'd wanted this to be as quick and painless as possible. She'd tried to anticipate his every move to stall this conversation. He'd want a drink, or he'd be hungry. Would she have a snack? She had his tea and pie sitting on the table waiting for him.

Now maybe they could get down to business.

"Well, what do we need to talk about?" Rose asked anxiously.

Thorn looked at her and replied, "Do you still have that antique brass bed your grandmother gave us?"

Rose was stunned. What did that have to do with forty years ago? "Yes, I still do. It's set up in the guest room."

"I was just thinking of how difficult it was to get comfortable until—"

Rose immediately interrupted him. "Thorn, we didn't come here to discuss our sleeping habits from our brief marriage."

"I don't remember getting much sleep back then." He bored into her with his obsidian eyes, and he smiled until Rose turned her head away.

"I didn't invite you here for a walk down memory lane. I thought you said you had some questions you wanted answered. But if this is what you came to discuss, you need to finish your pie and leave."

"Whenever I see a lemon pie, I always think of you, sweet and luscious with a bite to it." Thorn took a bite of the pie and slowly brought it to his lips. He grinned as he swallowed it, followed by a gulp of tea.

Rose crossed her arms. She would have to wait him out. No one ever rushed Thorn or pushed him into anything he didn't want. Finally, he took his last swallow of tea.

"THANKS, ROSE PETAL. That was good."

Thorn stared at her a moment, thinking a thousand thoughts about how he wished life had been different, but cold reality had brought him here. He needed answers; he needed closure.

But would it be possible, if he still loved and wanted that person as much as ever? He'd reached that conclusion about his own feelings only hours after seeing her again. The desires and aches that had driven him then were still there.

He knew his heart had to have answers, no matter the outcome. He braced himself for what she might say, and he let his biggest question roll off his tongue.

"Rose Petal, did you want to marry me, or did you do it only because you were pregnant and felt a responsibility for the baby to have a last name?"

Thorn finally had his cards out on the table.

ROSE STARED AT him, and she was totally shocked. She couldn't imagine he'd even ask that. She chose her words carefully. There could be no mistake in her reply.

Softly, she let her words escape, "It was because of my love for you that I wanted to marry you and have your baby. Thorn, you were my world back then. That was why I was so devastated when you left me. I knew then you'd only married me out of obligation and not love. Then, when the baby was stillborn, you'd found your opportunity, and you used it as an excuse to leave."

Rose finished almost inaudibly, but she didn't cry. She wouldn't cry. She'd done all that forty years ago. These were just fragile memories dragged out of her past.

She waited in the silence for a response, and when she looked up, she noticed the appalled expression on Thorn's face.

"Rose, stop and repeat what you just said about me leaving you. Say it again real slow. I want to make sure I heard you right. Don't leave out any details. Start at the hospital."

"Your parents came in the hospital room and told me the baby was stillborn, and the only reason you married me was because I was having your baby. Since the baby didn't survive, you wanted nothing to do with me. The biggest favor I could do their son was to honor his wishes and leave him alone.

"They said they'd take care of any incidentals regarding the death, and they hoped they never saw me again. Your mother insisted how much better off everyone would be this way.

"Then a nurse walked in and asked her to leave, so I could get some rest, explaining that I'd been through a hard ordeal. The nurse checked my vital signs and went to get me some water. You suddenly appeared and acted like everything was fine. You just wanted to give me a little good-bye kiss.

"I was almost hysterical at that point. I was distraught over the loss of our baby, then your mother being so cold and dismissive about it made me hurt all the more. At that moment, I never wanted to see your face again. I'd just lost our baby, and instead of you being supportive and caring, you walked away like nothing had happened. All you wanted was a good-bye kiss from me.

"In my heart, that was the last thing I would ever give you."

# — 32 —

THORN COULDN'T HAVE appeared more alarmed if someone had just hit him in the head with a baseball bat. He looked glassy-eyed and almost like he was about to pass out. Rose could immediately see something was terribly wrong.

"Thorn, are you okay? What's wrong? Do you want me to call 9-1-1?"

He made no response, just kept staring ahead. After a couple of seconds, Rose became anxious. She tried to talk to him again.

"Thorn, answer me. Are you okay?"

He collapsed against her, almost pushing her off her chair. He made a deep, heaving, moaning sound. He remained motionless, but Rose could feel his warm breath against her neck. Finally, he spoke in a slow and labored way, as if suffering from great pain.

"Oh, Rose Petal, my sweet, precious Rose Petal. Never did I want to be divorced or away from you, never!" He growled intensely as he kept his head buried in her shoulder.

Rose listened in complete surprise. That wasn't what his parents had told her.

Thorn slowly raised his head to gaze into Rose's eyes. "Rose, our baby wasn't stillborn. Roseanna is your daughter. My parents came out of the hospital room and told me you didn't want to see the baby, and you hated me for ruining your figure and your life. They also said you never wanted to see me again. That was why I was so desperate to get in to see you. But when I was finally able to go to you, the damage was done. You hated me; I could see it in your eyes. But I hoped that if I could get close enough to kiss you, it would be okay. I just wanted to touch you and make everything the way it was before. I wanted us to be a couple. I wanted us to raise our baby together.

"Instead, my parents raised her until their deaths when she was fourteen. By then, they had poisoned her against you forever. That's become my greatest fear. I was so lost and hurt without you, I signed up for military service. I didn't care what happened to me at that point. It was only when I got back and saw your sweet face reflected in our child that I could feel anything at all."

Thorn took Rose's hand and pressed it to his face. It was only after several minutes that he went on.

"Oh, baby. If I'd only known, I promise I'd have never left you. I didn't realize how mean and vindictive my parents were until it was too late. Even with Roseanna, they tried to poison her against me. They wouldn't let her come and live with my second wife and me. Roseanna was eight, then. But it was just as well. The marriage only lasted a couple of years. I couldn't seem to get you out of my head. At night I'd wake up saying your name. My second wife didn't appreciate that. She wanted more than I had to give."

By then, Rose was in shock. "Don't lie to me, Thornton Jebulon Wilder, not about this. Please don't lie to me," she pleaded, tears flooding her eyes, as she searched his face for some kind of revelation. Even without his words, she could tell from his haggard expression he was telling the truth as he knew it.

This changed everything and, even so, it changed nothing. The damage was done forty years ago. How could anyone have been so cruel? Why would anyone want to hurt a young girl who was in love with the only man she'd ever desired? Now all she could do was regret what might have been. Her shoulders drooped as large, salty tears slipped down her face and chin.

Thorn pulled her hand to his lips, and as he kissed it, she clung to his hand. She began to sob with the pain of all the years gone so wrong.

"Oh, Rose Petal, baby. Please don't cry, baby. Please don't. I didn't know, honest. I would have never left you, no matter what my parents tried to do." Thorn brushed the moisture from her warm, tear-stained cheeks. Rose couldn't resist him. She needed him. She leaned in to him, in an action brought on by desperation and hope.

Thorn brushed his lips against hers, before pulling away. "Rose, this isn't what I want. I want a real relationship with you. Not the one we had when we were kids, but a mature takes-whatever-life-brings-us kind of relationship. And as hard and difficult as this is, I should leave now. But I want you for now and forever. I realized it when I kissed you at the airport; I've never truly stopped loving you. I'm as impassioned by you now as I ever was. I'm not prepared to lose you, and I want our relationship to be right this time. I also want to have God's blessing and guidance in our lives. We still have a lot of obstacles to conquer. You and I have several questions about us to resolve. In addition, there's our daughter as well as our future together."

Rose knew he was right. He made her feel like no other man had ever made her feel. All the years of dealing with his rejection had made her insecure and lonely. She didn't even believe in true love anymore. She had thought that was what she and Thorn had shared when they were young. Then, it had been cruelly shredded before her eyes in the hospital, in as cold and calculating a way as possible. Now she was afraid to consider loving again, but she wanted to.

She struggled with the idea they could have a daughter, as the doctor had said the baby was stillborn. As she held Thorn's hand, she tried to recall everything she could about that fateful day. She only vaguely remembered the doctor. She'd been in so much pain, and then she'd been put to sleep.

Now that she thought about it, she only remembered Thorn's parents telling her about the baby being stillborn. She didn't remember the doctor saying that. She didn't even remember seeing the doctor after the delivery. Was Thorn's version of what happened the truth? Had his parents lied?

Surely there was proof of this somewhere. There had to be an answer to all these questions.

"The birth certificate, Thorn. I have to see the birth certificate." Rose spoke softly, as she moved away from him, giving her bruised emotions a chance to recover.

"What, Rose Petal? What about the birth certificate?" Thorn released her as she moved.

Rose looked him directly in the eyes and insisted, "I need to see our baby's original birth certificate. I never got a copy. I requested one several times. It was always the same response, that no such record had been documented. Now I want to see exactly what happened that cold January day. I want real answers from you, Thorn, before I'll ever believe Anna is my child. I want to believe it. I really do. But I must see the proof and then figure out how a doctor could pull off such a thing in a hospital. Before we get any further along, I need some answers, for my peace of mind. I must have them! Better yet, I want a DNA test run. I can't live with this uncertainty in my heart. I have to reach a conclusion about all this, one that I can accept."

Thorn replied, "So do I, Rose Petal. So do I."

# — 33 —

THORN LEFT ROSE'S house more confused than when he arrived. He had solved no problems. He'd only created more for himself. He was certain Anna wouldn't consent to a DNA test, not as angry as she was at Rose. Then, he'd practically told Rose he was still in love with her, but she hadn't returned his feelings, not verbally.

He wanted her to love him. He knew he couldn't be in the same room without wanting her. He also realized that if he was ever going to have a chance with her, it would take time and effort to prove his love and win her trust.

He was certain there was still a spark between them. He wanted to be with her, and she must want to be with him, at least in some small way. Where there was a spark, a flame could be fanned. At the picnic, just touching hands had energized them both.

But it would take more than sparks to set their love ablaze. Thorn would need to find cold hard evidence, facts that would possibly change how he felt about his parents, and possibly alter Anna's life forever.

His daughter might not find it in herself to forgive him, but like Rose, Thorn had to know the truth, and Anna needed to know as well.

IN THE SECURITY of her Austin stone home outside Round Rock, Rose sat in the deepening shadows of the late evening recounting the day's events. This hadn't been a typical Sunday by any means. Thorn had become a Christian, which alone was a wonderful, miraculous occurrence. But then to hear Thorn say their baby hadn't died was more than Rose could fathom. How many times had she thought that if only their child had lived, then maybe she and Thorn would have stood a chance, no matter how rocky their marriage had started?

Later, when she gave birth to Gill, Jr., she couldn't even answer the doctor's questions about her previous delivery. She'd explained to him how large the baby had been, and due to her own small size, she had been put under a strong anesthetic. She'd been in agony for days before she finally delivered.

Now to be told that her baby had survived and was alive was almost too much for Rose's heart and brain to absorb. She'd seen Anna, and yes, she did look like her, but her mind was unable to accept Anna as her child. Too many years of suffering with the pain and loss of her baby interfered. Rose knew she had to find the truth.

The sun was shining outside, and the dappling shadows sprinkled the last of the evening light across Rose's living room. She had no lights on yet, and the gathering gloom was a perfect muse to Rose's meandering thoughts. As she sat in her suede side chair, the phone rang.

"Yes, this is Rose."

"I made it safely. I'm home"

"Jenny?" Rose glanced at her phone to see her friend's name on the Caller ID window.

"Of course, it's me. What's wrong, Rose?"

Rose shared with her the information Thorn had told her earlier in the day. "Jenny, I gave him up for forty years. I was devastated by a man I loved with all my heart. Now I find he felt the same way about me. We never knew."

Rose wiped the tears from her face, as silence filled the phone.

Jenny whispered, "Rose, what are you going to do?"

"I can't trust him, Jenny. I can't throw away forty years of distrust in one weekend. I hate it that I still feel attracted to him, but I must admit I do. Yet, I have this snake of hate in my stomach tearing at me each time I'm around him. You know, like yin and yang."

"Yin and yang, Rose?"

Rose laughed, but it was one of near hysteria, not humor. "I'm sorry, Jenny. An old college term. Opposites. That's me. My heart wants Thorn, and I have four decades of distrust inside. No, I have four decades of hate that I've boxed up and pushed into the back corners of my mind. Now that man is trying to rip those boxes open, and I'm afraid of what might come out."

As the shadows in Rose's living room deepened, a light in the tree outside her window clicked on. Moments later, a small table lamp in the front hall came on as a timer attached to the plug shifted position.

Muted light filtered around Rose, creating a cocoon of light to cradle her distress.

"I need proof, Jenny. Not just Thorn's assurances. I told him I wanted a DNA test. Oh, Jenny. Forty years wasted. What if they didn't have to be thrown away? I loved Gill, Jenny, and I won't take that away from him. However, I should have been with Thorn all those years."

"Have you spoken to God about it? You've told me how much you trust His protection on your life."

Jenny listened as Rose did just that.

"God, please give me guidance. I've been without direction for two-thirds of my life. If Thorn's parents did this, I have no recourse against them. I only have you. I love this man, and I also know love cuts like a knife. Right now, he's slicing out my heart."

"Rose, honey," Jenny cautioned. "What if Thorn's telling the truth?"

"Jenny, I don't know. I told him I needed proof before we took our relationship anywhere." Rose sniffled as she gathered her emotions underneath her fragile shell of self-control and security.

Jenny was silent for a moment. Then she pressed Rose, "How does Thorn plan to prove all this, if it's really true? His parents are dead, and that military hospital has been closed for years. What does Thorn have to even start on?"

Rose replied in a hushed tone, "He's got her original birth certificate signed by the attending physician. Thorn said he would start from there and see if he can locate the doctor, if he's still living. From what I remember, he was fairly young at the time."

"When, Rose?" Jenny asked with bated breath. "I can barely stand the idea of waiting. I've seen you and Thorn together, and this weekend, you two needed each other like ice cream needs chocolate."

"Thorn plans to get this started first thing tomorrow. Oh, Jenny, I could have had a daughter and a son. This really boggles my mind to think about it. And if it's true, it also makes me angry and hurt to know this was kept from me. Back then all I ever wanted was for Thorn to love me and for us to be a family. Perhaps because of his parents, all that was taken from me."

Rose paused, crushed by the thought, and she had nothing more to say.

Jenny broke the silence. "I'm astounded by all the information you just shared. If all this is true, it could change yours and Thorn's future course in life. Rose, this is something you've got to find out as soon as possible. But I feel like Thorn is telling you the truth about your daughter. All of us at the reunion could see the resemblance she bore to you. She's a carbon copy, only in a larger size, Thorn-style. I don't think there's a way to duplicate that much of you without being related. I'm pretty sure she's yours."

Rose couldn't agree totally, being barely able to allow the possibility it might be true. "Maybe time will tell," was all she could say.

"Honey. Rose. This will work itself out. I'll call you next week and the next. I promise it won't be nearly a year like last time."

Rose laughed at their promise to call each other weekly. She agreed and whispered good night.

Rose got ready for bed, read her Bible, and said another prayer to God asking him for his guidance and direction. She asked for wisdom on how to handle the coming days ahead. She then laid down in her king size bed and attempted to sleep.

ON THE OTHER side of town, Thorn was trying to do the same. His prayer had been a little more desperate in nature. However, his spirit was sincere. Yet, as he lay in the darkness, sleep didn't come.

Both hearts were longing for the other, neither of them satisfied to be alone again.

# — 34 —

THE NEXT FEW days passed in a blur. Thorn was online contacting various websites for more information about verifying his daughter's birth, including information on DNA tests. His number one method, he discovered, sh
ould be to visit the county seat.

He also reviewed local birth announcements from nearly forty years before, as well as hospital records that had been digitized. The records clerk at the courthouse was his best ally, and he ordered and received a certified copy of Anna's birth certificate.

He called Rose and asked her to meet him.

He studied the document as he made the drive to Rose's house. *Roseanna Joy Wilder, born January 10.* It was stamped and notarized by Bell County and the state of Texas. It had been filed at the courthouse almost two months after the birth, which seemed very odd. But since she'd been born on the military base and not in the local hospital, there could have been a delay in transferring the records, according to the records clerk.

Thorn stood nervously at Rose's door, as he rang the bell and waiting for her to answer. He was unsure how she would react. She'd doubted what he knew was true, that Anna was her daughter, and he hoped the birth certificate settled things in her mind.

"Thorn? Come in." Rose swung the door back, and she stepped aside to give him plenty of room.

"Thanks, Rose Petal." Thorn nodded his head respectfully and stepped past gingerly, hoping to keep on her good side, at least until she read what he had in his pocket.

He held his breath as Rose read the document placed in front of her. The mother was listed as Rosemary Josephine Penndel Wilder, age 18, a housewife. The father was Thornton Jebulon Wilder, age 18, a welder. The baby's weight was 10 pounds and 4 ounces, all there in black and white. The doctor's signature was difficult to read, but it appeared to be a Dr. James Allen.

It was a validation of everything Thorn had said.

ROSE STARED AT the paper as if it were invisible, and she shook her head. She kept repeating the words, "I never knew. I never knew." Tears formed in her eyes. All this time she'd lived with a loss that never existed. Yet, for her it was still a loss, because she never had the joy of experiencing her daughter's life. How could a doctor allow such a thing to happen, to let someone believe her baby had died?

She smiled a bitter smile. "At least you gave her the name I picked out for her. I thought she would be such a joy in our lives, sealing our love forever. Never did I think she would tear us apart." Rose sniffled and patted her eyes with a tissue.

"She didn't tear us apart. It was my parents," Thorn responded vehemently. "They threatened to roast me for naming her Roseanna. They wanted her to have no part of your name. But she was my child, and I insisted. So the name she has is from us, not them."

Rose gave a wan smile, the best she could do in the catastrophe that had enveloped her. At least Anna had grown up with her father's love. She'd always hoped Thorn would be a good father. But when he rejected her because of the death of their baby, she'd doubted him. Then he was deployed across the ocean, and Rose was sure he'd come back a mess if he came back at all. He certainly wouldn't be father material after fighting in battle. Now she was glad she'd been wrong. He told her his military service made him appreciate the life he had back home. He'd loved his daughter and been a good provider for her.

With the truth from the birth certificate in her hands, Rose could finally let the truth soak in, and she found it empowering. She was ready for the truth to be revealed. She, as Rosemary Wilder, had given birth to a healthy baby girl. In addition, her daughter was alive. She wanted to call Jenny, Gill, Jr., Roxanne, and the whole world just to let them know she had a daughter and a son.

Rather than rejoicing, Thorn cautioned her.

"Rose Petal, I'm not sure Anna is ready for this. From our conversation the other day, she still doesn't believe me, and for good reason. She did live with my parents all those years. She thinks you abandoned her and wanted nothing to do with her. It'll be a lot of hard work before we can convince her otherwise.

"She's always known about you. You're the one that's the victim here. We didn't know it, but you were innocent. I should have seen it ages ago, but I was so blinded by the hurt and agony over losing you that I never considered my parents being at the bottom of it.

"I had no idea they were that malicious. I knew they didn't like you, but it never crossed my mind they would go to the extreme they did. However, we can't pull those years forward and relive them. The damage is done, and now all I can do is pray that God will help Anna understand and believe the truth."

Rose slowly nodded her head in agreement. She agreed with everything Thorn had said, and she only hoped she could learn to trust him again.

She had started, but it would be a long road for Rose, as well as for their daughter.

# — 35 —

ANNA HUNG UP her cell phone. Her dad had gone nuts. He was telling her that Rose had never known about her, and he was trying to convince her that her grandparents had lied to her.

Now he wanted her to submit a sample for a DNA test to prove she was who she said she was. It was crazy! How could anyone not know about her own baby and whether she'd lived or died?

After forty-five minutes on the phone with him, Anna simply disconnected the call. She'd had enough. That he was still in love with her mother was obvious, but to try to make up a lie just so they could all be one big happy family? Well, that was over the top, and Anna wouldn't hear of it.

She had never known him to be like this, so irrational. But that was what Grandmother had said when Anna was twelve, that Rose had some kind of power over her father that no one could conquer.

Anna had innocently asked what her mother was like and why they didn't like her. She could still see the reddening of her grandmother's face as she spoke.

"We got you out of there just in time. She didn't want you, and she certainly didn't know anything about raising a baby. Why your father had anything to do with her, I'll never know. It's like she was a drug. He couldn't stay away from her no matter how we tried to keep them apart. We knew she wasn't good for him, but he wouldn't listen to us until it was too late. By then, she'd trapped him by getting pregnant with you. He wouldn't leave her then, not when she was in a family way. So we let him marry her, knowing it was the biggest mistake of his life. Her parents put on a little show of trying to blame your daddy, but we knew the kind of girl she was."

"Couldn't Grandfather have requested a different posting?" Even a twelve, Anna knew how the military machine worked.

"We thought of that. The problem, however, was she was pregnant with your father's baby, and there wasn't one thing we could do about it."

Ann remembered how, from that time on, her grandmother had reinforced how awful her mother was and how she'd used her dad. But from the conversation she had with him on the phone, it didn't sound like her dad believed it had been that way at all. It sounded more like her dad was trying to push this whole family thing on her.

He must really want her to like her birth mom to go to the extremes he was talking about.

Despite this newfound change in her father's attitude toward her mother, Anna knew the truth. It was her grandparents who'd sacrificed and suffered for her well-being. They had even remained stateside when offered a better position in the Philippines.

Anna had only been about eight at the time. Her father had been newly married for a few months when her grandfather was posted to Manila. At the last minute, changes were made, and her grandparents decided to stay stateside. According to her father many years later, it was because he intended to keep her with him, and they didn't want that.

They didn't like his second wife, Julia, any better than his first. Her grandparents were constantly finding fault with her. She'd been a bit of a socialite, and that had been interesting to her grandmother at first. But when she realized that she was only interested in what made her happy and not in the Wilder family values, her grandmother's taste changed. She refused permission for Anna to go over, unless her father was there. She wouldn't let Julia take her shopping or to the zoo or any other activities unless her father was present as well.

Her grandparents seemed to resent anything Julia did for her.

After their divorce, her grandparents seemed more

dominant than ever. When Anna's dad married the third time, they had nothing to do with that wife. She was a short, bossy woman, they said. But whatever the reason, Anna didn't see her father much during the brief, nine-month marriage. Anna was almost twelve at the time. After that, her father didn't marry again. It wasn't until her grandparents' death that Anna spent extended time with her father. The longest time she'd been with him before that was overnight, and that on rare occasions, maybe twice a year.

It would take more than her daddy saying her mother had wanted her. It would take cold hard facts, which she was pretty sure he wouldn't be able to supply, especially since her grandparents were the only ones at the hospital when she was born. Her daddy had dug himself into a hole he wouldn't be able to get out of, and all because of her mother, that Rosemary woman. She seemed to hold some elusive power over her father, just like her grandmother had said, and it hadn't diminished over the last forty years.

Anna rubbed her belly as she dressed for bed. She felt a great satisfaction knowing she had a new life growing inside her. It wouldn't be too much longer, and she'd have to tell her father. Her baby-belly was beginning to swell. But one thing she did vow to herself: She'd make sure her baby felt loved and wanted, no matter what it cost. She'd see to that. Whether the baby's father was involved in its life or not, she would make sure it never lacked for love and acceptance.

Feeling more resolved than ever, Anna climbed into her bed and rubbed her nicely protruding belly as she whispered, "Goodnight my little wild thorn. Your mommy loves you."

# — 36 —

"AND THAT'S WHY I did it. I'm not proud of myself, and I've had to live with the shame of my youth
and fear these forty years now. It's truly been a cross
to bear, but I've no one to blame but myself." Dr.
James Allen looked Thorn in the eyes as his hands
worked the pencil in his hand, revealing his anxiety at
admitting what he'd done.

Thorn sat completely dumbfounded.

It had taken almost a month, but he had finally located a Dr. James Allen in the Bethesda, Maryland,
area. After several inquiries, it was confirmed he'd
practiced in Texas forty years before. Further investi-
gation revealed he'd been the base doctor at the time
of Rose's delivery.

Eventually, he'd spent several years as one of the

doctors posted to the White House Medical Unit, responsible for the health of the White House staff and visitors.

That was all Thorn needed to pursue the truth. When he found the gentleman's address, he made plans to meet him, giving his name as Jebulon Thornton. He didn't want the doctor to be suspicious, in case he remembered the last name Wilder, because if Thorn's father was involved, which he strongly suspected, he didn't want the doctor to be put off from the beginning.

He scheduled their meeting on the pretext of interviewing him about his illustrious career and arranged to meet him in a local coffee house.

"How did you end up in Maryland when you started in Texas?" Thorn asked, after they were introduced.

Dr. Allen replied, "Well, I put in for a transfer, and it was granted. Texas was so desolate, and I was from the Chicago area. I had no desire to be there. So I transferred as soon as I could."

"You were awfully young to get such a transfer, weren't you? With America's military commitments across the globe, I thought all the young doctors were posting overseas. At least that's what I saw when I did my tour of duty." Thorn noticed how the doctor winced at the mention of military commitments and overseas postings.

The doctor paused, and he clasped and unclasped his hands. He took a deep breath before he replied.

"Yes, that's true, but I had a friend in the big brass section. He helped me out. You know how that is." He took a sip of water and gave a faint smile that quickly faded. He glanced down and traced the small circle of moisture from under his water glass with a bare fingertip.

Thorn questioned again, "So this friend in the military did you a favor. Did you have to do one in return? How did you pay him back?"

Thorn could read body language and knew the old man was uncomfortable with this line of questioning. He moved slightly as if getting ready to cut the interview short. Thorn decided to ask about Anna, regardless of the circumstances. He told the doctor his real name and watched him flinch at the name Wilder. He knew the old gentleman remembered his father.

He confronted him with the bizarre story of his daughter's birth. He pulled out her birth certificate to show him the evidence she'd been a live birth. The old doctor seemed to draw up even more and become wizened as Thorn spoke. He pulled a crisp white handkerchief out of his pocket and dabbed his watery, faded blue eyes.

"I knew it was wrong, and I told the general I couldn't do it. I couldn't go back in and tell that young girl her baby had died. But he assured me I didn't have to. All I had to do was disappear for a few days. He'd see I got my transfer. He knew I was afraid of an overseas posting. So many of us went over there and never came back. Those rice paddies were our cemeteries. No one was returning. I was a scared kid, and the general used it to his advantage."

The old man wiped his face. It was hard for Thorn to watch him relieve those moments. Yet, Thorn also knew this was the only way he and Rosemary, along with Anna, could ever have closure to their past and a fresh start on a new beginning.

Dr. Allen continued, "I never spoke to the girl having the baby. All I said after the delivery was, 'It's a girl,' and I left the room. I doubt the poor child even heard me, with the anesthetic she was under. I was afraid she wasn't going to make it, as large as her baby was. We had to break both of the baby's shoulders in order to deliver her. It was one of the most difficult deliveries I ever did."

The old doctor looked around, letting his eyes trace the ceiling tiles, as he recounted the harshness of his memories.

"I paid a price for what I did. I'm sure it was nothing compared to what the baby's mother endured. For years, that young mother haunted me in my dreams. I'd read or hear about a lawsuit brought on by an angry patient, and I'd panic that I could be next. I finally made peace with myself.

"After that, I never let politics or power rule my decisions. I learned a very hard lesson at a very young age.

"I'm sorry for the heartbreak it must have brought the baby's mother. But the general assured me that she was unfit to raise a child and would probably abandon it. He said he was doing the mother and the baby a favor. I had no idea what the result would be."

The old doctor sounded exhausted. He wiped his face once again, and he slipped the handkerchief into his pocket.

Indeed, there was a new peace in the doctor's appearance that Thorn hadn't noticed before. Maybe this was what he'd needed, to tell someone about the horrendous mistake of his youth and get it off his chest. He'd carried that burden far too long.

Thorn thanked him for his time, and assured him there were no ramifications from his past coming to haunt him, if he'd do one thing for him. Thorn pulled out an envelope with hair from his daughter's brush back at the hotel in Austin. He just needed to get it tested for DNA and get home and tell Rose Petal the truth.

Then he'd have to tackle Anna. That would be the challenge, getting Anna to accept the truth and realize her grandparents had lied.

# — 37 —

ROSE WAS SURPRISED by the information Thorn had obtained. She knew she should have expected it; since he'd made this his mission, she knew he'd eventually uncover the truth. He had the sworn affidavit by the attending physician that her daughter, Roseanna Joy Wilder, had been a successful live birth, as well as a promise of a DNA test for further proof. In addition, he'd implicated his parents of lying and fraud to take the baby.

Rose knew now in her heart that Anna was indeed her daughter. She also realized from everything Thorn had told her that it would be a daunting task to convince Anna that Rose hadn't known about her existence. Despite that, Thorn said he was determined to make her understand, no matter what.

He also said some other things that had Rose's heart in a flutter.

"Rose Petal, now that you know the truth, how do you feel towards me?" He asked her that as soon as he finished telling her everything the doctor had said.

"I feel relieved to know you didn't leave me and join the military because I made you angry," Rose answered him softly.

"Baby, I went to the other side of the world to forget about you abandoning me and our daughter. I couldn't stand the thought of living without you in my life." Thorn reached for Rose. She laid down the official documents from the doctor, and she placed her head on his shoulder as he put his arms around her.

"Rose, I never want anything to come between us again, and I mean anything, including our daughter. It will take some convincing, I'm sure. I believe that eventually she'll have to accept the truth. But whether she does or not, I can't lose you again." He searched out the depths of her eyes, and she fell into his in pursuit of the happiness that should have been theirs.

ROSE FELT THE temperature rise, and she listened and understood exactly what Thorn was saying. He wanted to be with her, not because of guilt or a pregnancy, but because he truly cared about her. She buried her head in his shoulder and whispered, "I feel the same way, too, and I don't want to ever go through this feeling of loss again. Now that I know the truth,

I'm open to loving you. It's what I needed all along. If I'd only known, I'd have never let them take our baby. I'd have stayed married to you regardless of what your parents said or did. I just didn't know. My parents thought it was odd they got sent to Germany so soon after coming home from South Korea. Dad had only been in the states eighteen months when we shipped out again. Now I wonder if it was your parents trying to separate us even more. With me in Germany and them in Japan, there was no way for me to know anything about the baby. I wrote for a death certificate before we left but never received one. Now, the entire blur is beginning to make sense."

Rose once again felt the agony of the loss swell up inside. This time, however, she had Thorn to help her through it.

"I believe you're right, Rose Petal, and my parents were behind all of the trauma during our break-up and separation. They couldn't stand for me to make my own choices. They were convinced you wanted a promotion for your father, even when I told them you'd never mentioned it." His voice shook with emotion. "Oh, Rose Petal. If only I'd known how you really felt back then, none of this would have happened. My parents had me so jealous and anxious, I couldn't think straight. I constantly worried about losing you. And then my worst fear came true. When that happened, I lost all hope.

"It wasn't until I returned from my last posting and saw how beautiful our daughter was that I even wanted to live. She looked so much like you, I had to love her. Of course, my parents caused problems with her in every way they could. But upon their deaths, Anna had no choice but to live with me. Sadly, a lot of emotional damage had already been done.

"It took a couple of years before she completely trusted me, and I was her father. My parents made me out to be a near-mental case. They told her not to believe anything I said unless she confirmed it with them first. Only now do I see how vindictive they were."

Thorn pulled Rose closer. She didn't resist but instead reached to put her arms around him as she said, "We have to be a family, Thorn. I want that for us and Anna."

Thorn replied, "I do, too, Baby Rose Petal. I do, too."

THAT NIGHT, AS Rose thought about the day and her future, she thanked God for all He had brought about in her life because of her class reunion. As she climbed into bed, she said a prayer for her daughter, as well. During her sleep, the dream she'd had so often returned. She was in the hospital, the doctor said it was a girl, and then he seemed to disappear.

The next morning when Rose awakened, it was as if a fog had been lifted. She remembered hearing the doctor and even saw his face in her memory. She realized her subconscious had tried to tell her all these years that she did indeed have a daughter.

Now she had to convince Anna of the truth. Before that could happen, though, it was time to tell Gill, Jr.

She reached for the phone and began to punch in his number.

# — 38 —

ANNA WASN'T HAPPY about the situation, about her father coming to see her, or his insistence that he visit with Anna and bring along his first love.

She couldn't bring herself to say *her mother*. No, that woman wasn't her mother. She'd never had a mother. Her only mother had been her grandmother, and she'd died when Anna was fourteen. Since that time, there'd been no mothering influence in Anna's life. She was certainly able to do without one now.

She had to resign herself to accepting that her dad had never gotten over his first wife, even during those years they'd been apart. He'd dated during her growing up years and even married, appearing to genuinely care about each of the women he'd been involved with.

Yet, nothing compared to how he'd reacted that weekend around his first wife. In just the short time Anna observed them together, it was like her father had become a changed man. He seemed to hang on her every word and treat her as if she were some precious, fragile, priceless piece that could break at any moment if not given constant attention.

He'd never come close to treating any of the other women in his life that way.

The two of them seemed to understand what the other one wanted and how to influence each other to get it. It was like they'd never been apart. They could effortlessly read each other.

As much as she disliked the relationship, Anna could easily tell it wasn't one-sided, either. Her "mother" seemed as enamored with her father as he was with her. Now they were trying to force their rekindled romance on her.

She wanted nothing to do with it.

Her grandmother had told her the truth over the years, and she didn't need some simpering woman to try to convince her otherwise. She'd set them straight as soon as they arrived. Her father might not like what she had to say, but he'd have to deal with it. She wasn't being taken in by this woman's lies or deception. She wasn't a sentimental fool, and she'd let them know it as soon as they arrived, which would be any moment.

The doorbell rang, pulling her from her downward spiral in her bitterness towards Rose. As she opened the door, she was surprised to see her estranged husband standing at the door with roses in one hand.

"What brings you here?" She questioned him, harsher than he deserved, and she instantly regretted it. "I'm sorry, Sam. I was expecting someone else. We've been having family trauma, and you caught the edge of the storm. What are the flowers for?"

"Roses for my favorite Rose," he smiled, as he handed her the beautiful Tropicana-colored bouquet.

"Why, thank you!" Anna's face brightened. "You know how much I love this color. Let me get a vase." She was surprised to see Sam, although she was pleased. She went toward the kitchen for a vase in which to put her flowers, glancing back at him to smile, before stepping through the door.

"Other than the flowers, what made you stop by?" Anna called. She was curious why he would just show up at random, especially since they'd separated weeks before. They planned counseling in hopes of saving their relationship once Sam's out-of-town job was settled, but that hadn't come about yet. In the meantime, she felt it was better this way, as she couldn't deal with the long-term relationship side of his working situation. At least they'd split on friendly terms. If he loved his job more than her, that would become apparent very soon, and they could move on with their separate lives.

As she filled the vase with water, she thought of the baby. Until she was sure of why he'd come by, she needed to be cautious what she said around him.

Before he had time to answer, the doorbell rang again.

"Excuse me for a just a minute, okay?" Anna made her was back to the front hallway, handing him the flowers and the half-filled vase.

This time it was her parents and an older gentleman standing outside her door. She had no idea who he was, but she welcomed all three of them into her home.

"Dad, welcome in. Your two guests, too. I've got someone here for you to meet." It was turning out to be quite a party. Her father wouldn't be expecting Sam, who was in the dining room settling the flowers into the vase.

"Thank you, Anna." Thorn took her hand, at first hesitantly, then tighter when she didn't push him away. He leaned in and kissed her on the cheek, whispering, "I have someone for you to meet, also."

Anna made the introductions on her side. "Daddy, you know Sam, and Sam, this is my father's first wife, Rose Pet . . . I mean Rosemary." She faltered on the name. She had heard her dad call her that too often.

Sam looked at Rosemary and then back at Anna, and he gave a short laugh. "I can see the resemblance. This must be your mother, Anna. You look almost exactly alike. It's nice to meet you," he said, as he shook water off his hand and reached to shake.

"The pleasure is all mine," Rose replied, smiling at the tall, handsome young man, and taking his hand.

Anna looked at the older man, wondering why he was there, but certain it probably had to do with her in some way.

"Daddy, I don't believe I've met your friend," Anna said politely, turning to the distinguished older gentleman.

"Oh, honey. Let me reintroduce you to the first person who ever saw you. Dr. James Allen, please meet my daughter, Roseanna Wilder." Thorn made the introduction, while watching the expression on his daughter's face.

Anna said, "Oh! Well, it's nice to meet you, and I'm sure they've brought you here for a reason. Won't you all come in and sit down?" She turned abruptly as she led them toward the living room.

Dr. Allen began to explain as he followed her, "Yes, at my insistence, I convinced your father to let me tag along. I'm here to set the record straight once and for all. I was the attending physician at your birth almost forty years ago."

Anna stopped, looked at Sam and asked, "Do you think we can talk some other time, Sam? This is a family meeting, and I'm afraid it's an awkwardly private matter."

Thorn interrupted his daughter, "Anna, I'm the one who invited him. He is family, after all."

"Oh." She turned to face her father and gave him a sharp look. This seemed to be getting more complicated by the moment. "I didn't know. Then, let's be seated. Why did you invite Sam?"

"I just thought he should be here when the truth came out."

"The truth about what?" Anna asked, afraid she knew. Why else would a doctor from her childhood be sitting in her living room? She was the only one still standing, and she positioned herself on the edge of the sofa, ready to leap up if the answer wasn't what she wanted to hear.

"Your birth, of course," Thorn replied.

That was more than Anna could stand. It didn't matter who was in the room, and she stood and let her frustration fly.

"I already know the truth! Grandmother told it to me years ago. My mother abandoned me, period. That's the end of the story." She spat out the information like venom. She glared at Rose as if to dare her to dispute it.

It wasn't Rose who spoke. It was the old doctor.

"My dear, there was a terrible injustice done to this woman sitting right here." He pointed at Rose. "I delivered a ten-pound, four-ounce live baby girl. However, through a series of circumstances of which I'm not proud, this woman was led to believe the baby died."

Before he could go on, Anna blurted out, "How much is she paying you to say this? I know this isn't true. My grandparents were there and saw the whole thing." She glared smugly at the doctor.

"I know your grandparents were there. It was General Wilder who convinced me to do the horrible deed. He was my commanding officer at the time. He said he would keep me from being deployed to Cambodia or South Vietnam. Remember, we were still there until the late seventies. That was where I was afraid they were going to transfer me next. He told me he could use his rank to get me a position stateside. I accepted the bribe. It's something I'm not proud of. That's why I came all this way, to try to right a wrong that should have never happened. Your mother almost died delivering you. You were too large. We tried to stop the birth, but she wouldn't let us. She was willing to sacrifice her life so you could live. It was a miracle she survived."

Anna stared at the older man. How could he say this? Why was he trying to make her believe a lie?

Dr. Allen continued, "I know you may have some doubts, but here's my physician's card from my billfold. Here's my driver's license. And you can check my military record to see I was stationed at Fort Hood where you were born. I've no reason to lie. What I want to do is to clear my conscience, so I can live out my days in peace." The doctor stopped talking, and he pulled out a report from his pocket. "If you still have doubts, this should clear them up. I have a DNA report I've had run, and there's no doubt you and your mother are a perfect match."

She took the paper and looked over it, before looking to Rose, then cutting a hard look to her father.

"I think I should sit. I don't feel well." Anna swayed on her feet, and she was relieved to feel Sam at her side. She let him help her to the sofa. Her face felt warm, and her stomach was nauseated.

"You don't look like you feel well; do you need a glass of water? Sugar, when's your baby due?" Dr. Allen asked.

Suddenly, all eyes were on Anna. She felt herself growing hot. She glanced around the room uncomfortably. "Well, I, well, uh, I'm due in June," came out in a whisper, as her voice faltered.

"What?" Rose, Thorn, and Sam all said at once.

"You're pregnant? When were you going to tell me?" Sam was the first to ask.

"Another Little Wild Thorn. How wonderful," Rose murmured.

Anna's head shot around to Rose, "What did you say?"

Rose started to turn red from embarrassment. "It was just something I always called you before you were born. I called you my Little Wild Thorn," she finished quietly.

Anna shook her head. That was the same thing she said to her baby when she rubbed her belly each night.

The doctor spoke up, "Well, I've seen thousands of pregnant women in my years of practice, and a June due date isn't likely. I'd say you're further along than you think, or you could possibly be expecting twins."

"Twins!"

Now, everyone was talking.

# — 39 —

ANNA COULDN'T TAKE in everything the old doctor had told her. For the next hour, he quietly recounted the events that involved him and her birth. When faced with all the facts, along with the DNA proof, it added up. Her grandparents had lied to her, but why?

"They never wanted me in control of my life," her father answered. "They were afraid of losing me. My father controlled everything around him in the military; however, he didn't control me. By doing the things they did, they lost me anyway."

Anna was bewildered by the new information. The doorbell rang again.

"Who could it be now?" Anna muttered, as she opened it wide. She stared for a moment, unable to comprehend what she saw. Then she giggled. Standing in front of her was a man with her eyes and features; he even had her nose. He was about an inch shorter than she was and maybe five or so years younger. There was no mistaking him, though. He could only be her brother.

"You must be Anna," the man said with a smile, as he put out his hand.

"And you must be Gill, Jr." Anna answered him, with humor in her voice, as she shook his hand. "Won't you come in?" she offered.

"Thank you. I believe I will." Gill stepped through the door in his ostrich cowboy boots to see his mother and the man who was obviously Anna's father standing arm-in-arm. His mother reached out to greet him.

"Gill, honey. I'd like for you to meet Thornton Wilder, better known as Thorn."

"Well, I feel like I know you already, your mother speaks so often of you." Thorn removed his cowboy hat, put out his hand, and squeezed Gill's tightly. "I hope this is the beginning of many happy times we spend together."

"If my mother's happy, then I know it will be," Gill replied, staring at the man whom his mother had said was her first love. "Mom called and told me all about her youthful past. I admit I was surprised and shocked at first, but after I thought about it, I was also pleased." Giving Thorn a meaningful glance, he continued. "Now I won't have to worry about her being alone. From the looks of things, it's obvious she won't stay single much longer, which of course is fine with me."

THORN CALLED TO the people in the house, "I've asked everyone to be here today to help put my past with Rose Petal to rest. There were lies, sabotage, and deceit in our youth. We both lost our way. Despite everything, with God's help, we found the answers we were looking for and have come to terms with it." He looked at Rose and reached for her hand. "Now I'd like to start a new future with her as my wife. I'm asking my first and only true love to marry me, with God's blessing, and make me the happiest man on the face of the earth."

Everyone began clapping and smiling. Rose started crying, which made Anna start crying as well. She tried to hide it, but everyone saw the large, transparent teardrops coursing down her cheeks. She couldn't seem to help it.

"What is it, honey?" Thorn put his arm around Anna's shoulder. "Why the tears, now?"

"My father's finally going to be happy, and it took my mother to make him so." Anna brushed at her cheeks, and she chuckled. "It's obvious you two truly love each other. I no longer have any doubts about either of you. Look, even Dr. Allen has a tear or two in his eyes."

As she spoke, the old doctor reached for his handkerchief and began to pat his eyes.

Sam spoke up, "I think Anna and I need to talk in private. I think this may need to be a double ceremony. We need to renew our vows."

Anna's eyes opened wider than they'd been all evening.

"Anna, what's this about?"

"I haven't told you, Daddy. Sam and I have been separated, but I think we've worked things out."

Cheers went up from everyone as Sam and Anna walked toward her bedroom.

THORN LOOKED AT Rose as her eyes stared up at her one true love. She couldn't believe what had happened, all because of their class reunion.

This indeed had become a true reunion of the heart.

## *Did you like this book?*

**There's more!**

Read all three books in **The Reunion Series** by DeLora Conley-Walls.

## Trusting Heart Reunion

*(Out Now!)*

## Timeless Heart Reunion

*(Out Now!)*

## True Heart Reunion

*(Out Now!)*

**Find these and more at:**

THREE SKILLET
www.ThreeSkilletPublishing.com

and

*Amazon*

www.ingramcontent.com/pod-product-compliance
Lightning Source LLC
Chambersburg PA
CBHW060145130626
46556CB00006B/2500